HANDS OFF OUR SCHOOL!

HANDS OFF OUR SCHOOL!

by

Joan Lingard

Illustrated by Mairi Hedderwick

HAMISH HAMILTON
LONDON

HAMISH HAMILTON LTD

Published by the Penguin Group
27 Wrights Lane, London W8 5TZ, England
Penguin Books USA Inc., 375 Hudson Street, New York, New York 10014, USA
Penguin Books Australia Ltd, Ringwood, Victoria, Australia
Penguin Books Canada Ltd, 10 Alcorn Avenue, Toronto, Ontario, Canada M4V 3B2
Penguin Books (NZ) Ltd, 182–190 Wairau Road, Auckland 10, New Zealand

Penguin Books Ltd, Registered Offices: Harmondsworth, Middlesex, England

First published in Great Britain 1992 by Hamish Hamilton Ltd

Text copyright 1992 by Joan Lingard
Illustrations copyright © 1992 by Mairi Hedderwick

1 3 5 7 9 10 8 6 4 2

The moral right of the author and artist has been asserted

British Library Cataloguing in Publication Data
CIP data for this book is available from the British Library

ISBN 0–241–13261–4

Printed in England by Clays Ltd, St Ives plc

For Valerie Bierman

CONTENTS

Will Johnson   P7

Lynne Ramsay   P4   Alison Gordon   P6

John Simpson   P2   Jamie McCree   P3

GLEN FINDIE PRIMARY SCHOOL ROLL

Katy McCree   P6   Mairi McPherson   P7

Bruce Ramsay   P6   Danny McCree   P5   Mary Johnson   P4

Hector Gordon   P3   Elspeth Scott   P2   Annie McCree   P1

Blackberry Smith   P1

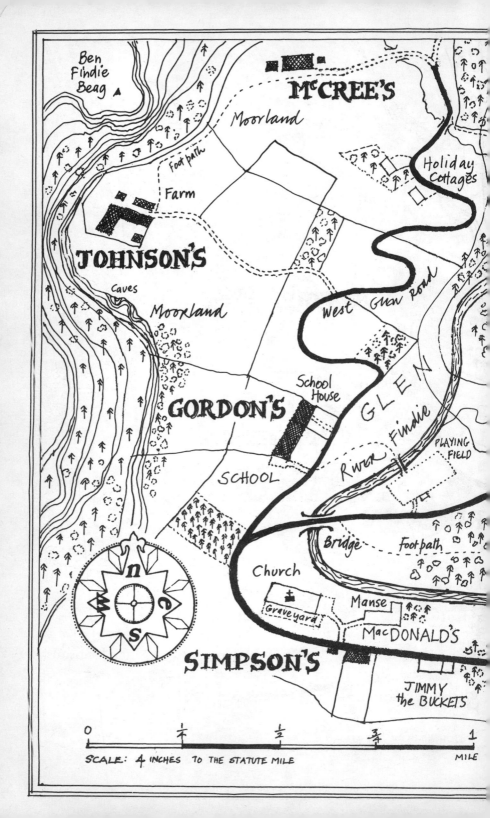

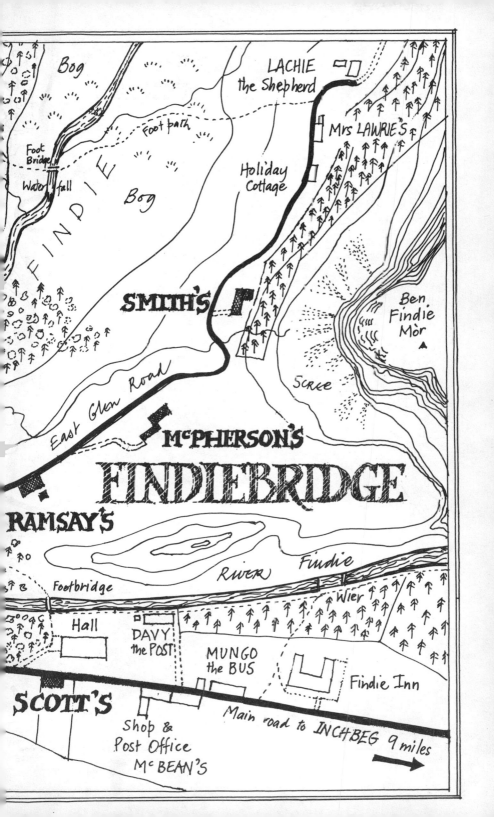

ONE

SMALL IS BEAUTIFUL

This is the story of our school, and I, Katy McCree, P6, am telling it. Now and then some of the others try to butt in and make suggestions and sometimes I put them down and sometimes I don't. It depends on how I'm feeling. And what they're saying.

Mairi McPherson, P7, who is looking over my shoulder, has just said, 'You're giving the wrong impression.'

'How am I?'

'If you say, "This is the story of our school," people will expect it to be the *whole* story. From the very beginning to the very end.'

'She couldn't tell the whole story.' That's Will Johnson, P7. 'It'd take till next year.'

He's right. Our school is more than a hundred years old. It was built in 1880: the date is set in stone over the door.

I can see that Mrs Gordon, our teacher, is pleased that I've got one fact down, at least. Facts are important, she's always reminding us. As well as using our imagination. She's keen on the imagination.

'I am going to tell the last part of our school's

story,' I inform them. 'The bit that's still going on. The most *important* bit of all.'

'The awfullest part,' says my brother Danny, P5.

No one could argue with that, not even Mairi McPherson, except of course to tell Danny that there's no such word as 'awfullest'. Mairi's good at arguing. If there were tests in it she'd score ten out of ten.

'Details, Katy,' Mrs Gordon is saying, 'give some details about the school and get a move on! And don't forget to give a rounded-out picture, warts and all.'

'And go back to your seat, Mairi!' she adds. 'How can anyone write if you're hanging over the top of them?'

I give Mairi a little smirk as she moves away. She narrows her eyes at me in return.

So here, then, are a few details:

Our school is called Glen Findie Primary School and, as you can see from the map at the front, it's in Glen Findie, which is in the Highlands of Scotland. The River Findie is a spate-river, which means that its level goes up and down. Sometimes, when it's in spate, swollen with spring or winter rains, it boils and foams. At others, when the level drops, it runs quietly over the smooth grey stones in its bed. The water is toffee-coloured from the peat. It starts up at the head of the glen in the higher hills where the deer go in summertime. There are grouse and pheasant up there, too, on the moors, and Danny says he's

14

seen a golden eagle. He might well have done as he's got eyes as sharp as tacks. We McCrees live up at the head of the glen so we're the first to get snowed in when there's a heavy fall. It doesn't snow *all* winter as some ignoramuses (who live in the South) seem to think. We don't *quite* live on the Arctic Circle!

There are two roads up the glen, one on each side of the river. They're never exactly busy. The school bus comes to collect us in the mornings and brings us back at night. Apart from that, you won't see much else on the road except for the Johnsons' orange tractor and the postie's red van or our families' cars as they rattle up and down to the village shop in Findiebridge.

The only time we have anything like a traffic jam is in summer when Will's father is moving his cows and they're straggling all over the road. The tourists tend to get impatient and lean on their horns. As if a few minutes would matter to them! There can be a problem too when the school bus meets the refuse truck on a tight corner. Then a lot of yelling goes on, with both drivers hanging out of their windows. Neither wants to back up. The chances are they'd get their back wheels wedged in the ditch.

'I've got a precious cargo on board,' shouts Mungo the Bus.

'I've got a heap of rubbish you wouldn't want strewn across the road,' roars Jimmy the Buckets.

We stick our heads out of the windows and join in.

(Put in some more details about the school, Mrs Gordon is telling me. So, OK, I'm just about to! Not that I say that to *her*.)

Our school is made of thick grey stone and has a

grey slate roof.

'The roof needs repairing,' says Will gloomily.

We *know* that. Don't we have Mrs Gordon's yellow
plastic bucket in the corner to catch the drips? And
Mrs Scott's red plastic basin by the far wall? (Mrs
Scott is the school cleaner, and mother of Elspeth,

P2.) Most days there are steady plop-plopping noises coming from both the basin and the bucket. When it's raining really hard – which it quite often seems to be – the plops build up until they're beating a steady rat-tat-too. This can give Mrs Gordon a headache. And it means that we have to keep getting up and down to empty out the water. Which *we* don't mind.

Our school has only one room, apart from the toilets, which don't seem to count as rooms. Not according to Will's uncle who's an estate agent in the town. But our one room is long and high and light. And it's painted white and has six windows, each with twelve panes. (How is this for details, Mrs Gordon?) Three of the windows face on to the road and the other three look on to the playground at the back.

On the other side of the dry stane dyke, which marks the school boundary, there's the field where Will's dad keeps some of his sheep. And beyond the field is the birch wood which is brilliant for hide-and-seek. It's jungly, and so thick in the middle that you can't see daylight. That's where the roe deer go. They leave their tracks on the paths between the trees. They speed away when they hear us coming and all *we* can hear is the fallen branches crackling under their feet. But on misty mornings they come out to the edge of the field to graze, and again when the dark comes creeping in.

Behind the wood the hill rises up, purplish-brown

on the lower slopes, with snaggles of dark green where a few firs are hanging on, and glittery white on top as if icing sugar has been dusted over it. In winter the hill's all white.

'Get a move on!' Alison is saying. 'You're supposed to be telling the *story*.'

'You keep getting sidetracked,' moans Mairi.

'Keep your hair on,' I tell them. 'I am just about to reveal ALL!'

TWO

OUR SCHOOL

It all began on the first day of the winter term when Mrs Gordon came in, picked up a brand-new stick of yellow chalk and wrote on the blackboard in large letters:

SMALL IS BEAUTIFUL

Then she laid the chalk in its groove, dusted her hands together and turned to look at us.

'What do you think *that* means? Small is beautiful?'

You might be able to guess whose hand would be up and flapping about!

'Well, Mairi?' asked Mrs Gordon.

'Small things are nice.'

We glanced across at the table where the Wee Ones sit. Blackberry was licking a red felt-tip pen and drawing on the backs of her hands. She was concentrating so hard that she hadn't heard. (Her mother and father are artists – that's probably why she's got a name like that. They've come up to live in the glen so that they can paint the hills and peat bogs and get away from the noise of traffic.)

Our Annie had heard Mairi, even though she had pulled up her trouser-leg and was picking at a scab on her knee. Blood was trickling out of it down into her socks. Clean on this morning.

'I'm nice,' she said, looking up from the scab. 'I'm very *very* nice.'

I couldn't let that pass. '*You* nice! You must be joking! She messed up all my best poster paints last night, Mrs Gordon. Would you believe it, she stirred them together with *cocoa*?'

'She did too, Mrs Gordon,' confirmed Jamie, his eyes solemn-looking and as round as marbles. 'I seen her do it.'

'Saw,' I corrected him, then looked back at the teacher. 'She's always messing my things around.'

Annie's bottom lip was trembling. She's good at putting it on. As my dad says, she likes to play to the gallery.

'That's enough of that now, Katy!' Mrs Gordon took up her long pointy wooden pointer and, putting the tip of it under each word on the blackboard in turn, repeated, 'SMALL IS BEAUTIFUL.' It was like she was saying it in ten-foot high capital letters.

'So, any more ideas, children?'

'I think maybe it means that not everything that is big is beautiful,' Will suggested.

'You're quite right, Will! You're quite right! Not everything that is big is beautiful, *or* necessarily good.'

We could see that our teacher was all hopped up about something underneath, although she was trying to stay cool on top. Her eyes were giving off sparks and her cheeks were flushed, as if she'd been for a brisk walk up the hill and back. We waited. Even Blackberry stopped drawing on her hands and

22

was staring at the teacher with her mouth half open.

'*Some* people,' said Mrs Gordon, leaning heavily on the 'some', 'think that unless something is big it can't be any good.'

'I like big balloons,' said Mary Johnson.

Surprisingly, Mrs Gordon looked pleased. 'But if they get too big they burst, don't they, Mary?'

'My daddy blew up my purple balloon with the green dinosaur on it and it burst,' announced John Simpson proudly. 'It got bigger and bigger and thinner and thinner. Then it went POP!' He smacked his hands together.

'Exactly! Now *some* people,' Mrs Gordon was getting wound up again, 'think that small schools are no good.'

That made us sit up straight.

'*Some* people want to close us down.'

Who were these *some people*?

'I expect they're from the Education Committee,' said Mairi knowingly. One had come to visit us a month or so ago. He'd been dressed in a navy-blue suit and shiny black shoes and he'd smiled at us as if he'd come to bring us a treat. But we knew he hadn't. He didn't take us in, not for one second he didn't. He'd come to look us over. To check up on us. We'd all been on our best behaviour, the Wee Ones too. Nobody slouched or swung their feet. And Annie had asked to go to the toilet only twice. I'd given her a good talking-to on the way to school.

She likes washing her hands and hanging over the basins and usually ends up with wet cuffs and a wet front.

'Splendid, splendid!' this navy-blue man had kept saying, when we answered his dead-easy questions. He'd seemed to think he should be asking something all the time. What is the capital of Scotland, children? What are nine fives? Who knows who Robert the Bruce was? He'd stood in front of the stove rocking backwards on to his black heels, flashing his not-very-white teeth at us. Mairi said afterwards that they looked like piano keys that had gone a funny colour. (Mrs Gordon of course had had to tick her off, but you could see she wasn't really annoyed.)

'*They* say', Mrs Gordon went on now, 'that *we* are too small. That it doesn't make sense to keep a school open for fourteen pupils.'

'Would that mean we wouldn't have to go to school?' asked Danny hopefully. Trust him! He'd spend all his time out of doors if he could. He likes going round with our dad who does odd jobs for people like fencing or building sheds. Or else he buys whole tree trunks from the Forestry and saws them up into logs on his big electric saw and sells them.

'Of course you'd have to go to school!' Alison flipped back her long, golden, *well-brushed* hair, which is quite unlike my sooty tangle. (All of us

24

McCrees are dark-haired and dark-eyed.) 'They'd send us to Inchbeg,' said Alison.

'Inchbeg!' we echoed. Inchbeg is our nearest town. It's nine miles from Findiebridge. We knew we'd have to go there eventually, for secondary school. (Will and Mairi would be going in the autumn.) But none of us wanted to leave Glen Findie before we had to.

Elspeth, whose tears spout if you as much as look sideways at her, began to cry. Maybe she thought we were going to be sent to the Tolbooth in the town. That's where they used to jail criminals in the olden days. We went to visit it one day. Mrs Gordon told us to imagine what it would be like if we were shut up in that grisly place with the wind blowing through the slits in the walls. With leg-irons on, too, more than likely, and not enough to eat. And all you might have done was steal a bag of spuds because you were hungry. We wrote it up as a part of a local history project afterwards. We've done projects on most things you can think of. And some that you probably can't. Like 'The Threat to the Capercailzie.' (Bet some of you don't know what a capercailzie is! Or how to pronounce it.)

Mrs Gordon told Elspeth that it was all right, there was no need to cry, no one was going to do anything nasty to her.

'I would say closing us down would be pretty nasty,' I growled.

'We could tell them we won't go,' said Bruce, who's not a great talker. He's good at shinty, though, he and Will, both, and they sometimes go into the town on a Saturday to play. (Shinty's a bit like field hockey, in case you don't know. But faster and rougher. And girls don't get to play. Which I don't think is fair. I can handle a shinty stick as well as any of the boys when we play in the field on the other side of the Findie.)

'A lot of good that would do!' said I. '*Telling* them!'

'We could tell them we *won't* go!' said Will.

'We could fight it!' I cried, and thumped my fist on my desk, the way my dad does on the kitchen table sometimes, when he and my mum are having an argument. It's usually about him going out to the Findie Inn. He'll say he'll only be half an hour and she'll say tell me another one.

The rest took up the cry. *Let's fight it!* Why should we let *them* take our school away from us?

We were all on our feet and making such a hullabaloo that we hadn't heard the door opening. Mrs Gordon had, however. She banged the pointer across her desk and shouted, 'Quiet, children! Seats!'

We quietened at once when we saw that the minister's wife, Mrs MacDonald, who's also our local councillor *and* a member of the Education Committee for our region, was standing in the doorway.

THREE

THE LETTER

'I can well understand you being worked up, children,' said Mrs MacDonald, as she settled herself on top of Mrs Gordon's desk and unbuttoned her sheepskin jacket. The desk creaked and swayed a little. Mrs MacDonald is not what you'd call 'light as a feather'. Her old fat spaniel Sam, who looks like a rug, lay down at her feet and began to snore. They usually stay for a while when they come. '*I* am worked up, too, let me tell you!'

That cheered us. If Mrs MacDonald, who was on the Education Committee, wanted to keep the school open, how could they go ahead and close it? I put up my hand and asked her.

'Well, you see, Katy, I am not the *only* person on the committee, as you well know! Unfortunately! If I were, it would certainly not close. But most of the others don't seem to agree. Of course, I was at school here myself – over forty years ago!'

A number of our parents and grandparents are old pupils of the school. Not incomers like the Smiths and the Scotts. The Smiths have been here only two years, and the Scotts nine. Mrs Gordon says we shouldn't use the word 'incomer', it doesn't sound friendly.

In 1900 there were forty pupils at the school. Over the years the roll gradually dropped until there were only fourteen of us. Some younger children – like my sister Florrie – were waiting to come when they would turn five. Not enough, though, to push the numbers up any higher.

(I'd told the rest of them that they should get their parents to have more children. After all we McCrees were doing our bit for the school, so why shouldn't they? Lynne Ramsay then went home and told her mother that I had said that *she* should have another baby! That fairly put the fat in the fire! Sparks were flying in the glen. Mrs Ramsay came steaming up to see my mother and I got a ticking off. And I was only trying to help! My mum says I've got too big a mouth for my own good. But what can you do about the size of your mouth?)

Mrs MacDonald sighed. 'Everyone these days wants to cut this and that. They want to shut the little places where people are happy and put them all together in a great big heap. They've got a big name for it. Rationalization – that's what they call it.'

Mrs Gordon wrote it on the blackboard underneath SMALL IS BEAUTIFUL

RATIONALIZATION

We older ones copied it into our jotters.

'It usually means doing something because it's

cheaper,' said Mrs MacDonald, 'and not bothering about the way people feel.'

'But what *can* we do?' asked Will desperately. 'Is there anything?'

'We're certainly not going to throw in the towel yet!'

I cheered. Mrs Gordon frowned to let me know I should be quiet. But not throwing in the towel seemed to me a cheering matter.

'My mummy doesn't 'llow me to throw the towel on the floor,' said Elspeth.

'Shush!' hissed Mairi.

'But she doesn't.' (It can sometimes drive you up the wall having the Wee Ones in with us Bigger Ones.)

'I'm going to call a meeting in the village hall,' Mrs MacDonald continued, 'and ask all your parents to come. You must tell them its *very* important that they *do* come.' (I'm sure she'd give them a ticking off if they didn't.)

'My mummy'll come,' said Blackberry. 'And my daddy.'

'That's good, Blackberry. And you children can do something too. You can write a letter to the Director of Education telling him that you want to keep your school.' Mrs MacDonald eased herself off Mrs Gordon's table and prodded Sam with her toe. 'Time to go, old boy.' He heaved himself up and ambled after her. Mrs MacDonald looked back from the door. 'Make sure you write a nice letter and explain why you want to keep your school. Try to get the Director to understand how you feel.'

The letter took years to make up. (All right, Mairi – hours! Mairi is a right nit-picker – you know what I mean? If you say you ate tons of chocolate on your birthday, she'll say, 'How could you eat *tons*? If you ate tons of anything you'd burst.') We kept putting things in and taking things out. And, needless to say, we had a few arguments along the way.

Danny wanted to say that he liked watching for deer, but we thought that would suggest we spend all our time looking out of the window and not working. Hector wanted to put in that his mummy would lose her job. I thought that fair enough – for she would – but Mrs Gordon said firmly that we must leave her out of it. (The Gordons would lose their house, too, as it goes with the school.) And Annie of course wanted to say that she liked the toilets!

After we'd done a few drafts, Mairi was picked to write out the final version. Her handwriting is the neatest and she never makes smudges. She went to wash her hands first. Annie went with her, saying that she needed the toilet.

This is what Mairi wrote:

Glen Findie Primary School,
Findiebridge

The Director of Education

Dear Sir,

We were very upset to hear today that our school is to be closed and are writing to ask you to think again about your decision.

Our school is a very fine school and we believe that we get an excellent education, just as good any of the pupils in the town, perhaps even better, because we can each work at our own level. The bigger ones help the little ones, and we are like one big family.

Our school has been here since 1880. Many of our ancestors were pupils. We have pictures of them on the wall which remind us of the way people lived in bygone days. We have done projects on the glen showing how it was in 1880, 1914, 1945 and 1980, and are doing one now on life here today. All the inspectors and advisers who have visited the school have praised our projects. They said that they showed a lot of imagination. They said that it was good to keep a link with the past and not to forget it. One lady inspector wrote the word INHERIT-ANCE on the blackboard. She told us that it was important not to lose sight of our INHERITANCE.

Each year we produce a school magazine and everyone from Primary One to Primary Seven writes or draws something for it. We always enter our magazine for the *The Scotsman* newspaper's School Magazine competition and last year we won prizes for the best 'Current Affairs' and 'Letters' categories. I expect you remember sending us a letter of congratulation? You said, 'It is a remarkable achievement for such a small school and proves that it is quality not quantity that counts.' Mrs Gordon pinned your letter on the wall and we copied what you had said into our jotters.

This year our magazine is going to be even bigger and better.

We love our school.

We are happy here.

We want to keep our INHERITANCE.

And so we ask you, please, sir, not to shut us down.

Yours sincerely,

We then all signed our names, Blackberry and Annie included, although it took Blackberry a few minutes to print all her letters. She huffs and puffs when she writes and sticks out the tip of her tongue.

'Hurry up!' I told her. 'We'll miss Davie the Post.'

'Now, Katy!' said Mrs Gordon. 'Remember – you were five once! And a right handful you were too. You wouldn't sit still.'

'She's not much better now,' said Will with a cheeky grin and leaned sideways in his desk so that I couldn't swipe him.

When Blackberry finally got the 'y' down, Will took the two sheets of paper and folded them carefully. We watched him put them into the long white envelope. Mairi then wrote on it the name and address of the Director of Education.

'Mr Big,' commented Danny. He thought for a moment, and said, 'Hey, maybe that's why he doesn't like little things!'

FOUR

THE SCHOOL MAGAZINE

'Postie, postie, bring our mail,
Postie, postie, can't you hear us wail?
Bring us a letter
And then we'll feel better,
So postie, postie, please bring our mail!'
Mary Johnson, P4

Her brother Will gave her the 'wail' but she wrote the rest herself. Mrs Gordon put the poem into the magazine folder which was getting bulgier every day.

Mary's poem told how we were all feeling. We were like cats on a hot griddle and couldn't sit still, especially when the hands of the wall clock were starting their big climb up to twelve noon. That's the time when we hear the postie's horn and then his van comes beetling round the corner. Davie looks a bit like a beetle himself, a nice beetle. He's small and dark. And he scuttles about, once he's out of the van. You never see him walking. He's always got a grin on his face though, which I suppose isn't too beetle-like.

Davie knew of course what we were waiting for. We could tell there was no letter the moment we saw his face. His mouth would be turned down at the corners, like commas. He usually has some mail addressed to Mrs Gordon or The Head Teacher, but our letter, when it came, would surely have our names on it: The Pupils of Glen Findie Primary School.

'It'll come one of these days.' Davie was doing his best to keep our spirits up. 'Letters take time.'

We'd sent ours First Class. That should only take a day to get there.

'Aye, but sometimes things get held up. And he might send his back Second.'

'And he might not reply immediately,' Mrs Gordon reminded us. 'He'll get masses of letters every day. You can't expect him to reply to yours first.'

We supposed he might even reply to it last of all.

It never seemed to stop raining either during those days when we were waiting. Heavy battering rain with a driving wind behind it which rattled the windows and kept the plops going in the basin and the bucket. We were up and down like yo-yos emptying them. That was about the only exercise we did get. We couldn't go out to play at break or lunchtime. It makes me feel twitchy when I have to sit still all day.

'Now you've got plenty to do, children,' said Mrs Gordon. 'There are just a few days left in which to finish the magazine.'

She suggested I include one or two of the entries here

(with the spelling sorted out) so that you can get an idea of what we put in it. I'll start with the Wee Ones.

Blackberry had drawn a fairy, complete with wand, wings and wellies. (She's good at drawing – you could see it was meant to be a fairy. She takes after her mother and father, I suppose.) Mrs Gordon had then helped her to write a story. (That's how the Wee Ones work.)

'I saw a fairy in the glen. Annie says I did not, But I did. I did saw it. It had a wand and wings and green wellies.'
Blackberry Smith P1

Our Annie had then drawn a witch wearing a hat and wellies and carrying a broomstick that was twice the size of herself. The picture was *very* black.

'I saw a witch in the glen. Blackberry says I did not. But I did so see it. It said hello to me. It had a black hat and black hair and black teeth and a black broom and black wellies.'
Annie McCree P1

Danny felt inspired to carry on their stories.

'The witch that Annie saw is really a bad fairy in disguise coming to shut down our school. The fairy that Blackberry saw is a good fairy who is coming to try to save us.

'They have met up by the burn. They are wrestling with each other. The witch is trying to push the good fairy into the burn. Her green wellies are slipping on the mud . . .

'Will the witch push the good fairy into the burn?

'Watch out for next week's episode . . .'

Danny McCree P5

'Danny always puts that in when he doesn't know how to finish a story,' complained Lynne. 'Watch out for next week's episode.'

'Well, we don't know yet who is going to win, do we?' he retorted.

I turned on him. 'We do so know! There's no question.'

'There is a question, isn't there, Mrs Gordon?' Danny went on colouring in his picture. He'd drawn the two fairies wrestling with one another. They looked more like henchmen of Robert the Bruce, with their big beefy arms and legs like tree trunks, and blood dripping everywhere. (Danny loves putting blood in.) Balloons were coming out of their mouths.

'Take that!' the witch was saying.

'You take that!' the good fairy was saying, as she punched the witch on the tip of her very, very, very, long, thin, pointy nose.

Mrs Gordon seemed to like Danny's picture. She was smiling at it at any rate. (You know, sometimes I think that, although she's a teacher, she's not got what my Auntie Jean would call 'good taste'.)

Mrs Gordon thought that we might be able to get some of the pictures colour-photocopied. 'It would cost more but it would improve the magazine.'

'Then everyone could see the blood,' said Danny gleefully.

We have a magazine fund. On Fridays, at lunchtime, we have a sale of baking and homemade sweets to raise money. People come from round about. The Ramsays always bring fudge – their mother's daft about fudge, all kinds, chocolate, vanilla, walnut, honey, whisky, raisin – and the Johnsons bring scones. The rest of us bring whatever we can, depending on what moods our mothers are in. I like making toffee, but sometimes it can be a bit hit-or-miss, I have to confess.

'Mostly miss,' giggled Alison. 'What about the lot that ran like syrup?'

'And then there was the time it was set like a rock and we nearly broke our teeth on it,' said Will.

What a cheek! That was the last time I'd give them any of my toffee.

I got up to empty the red basin. The water was nearly brimming over.

'Mind how you go now, Katy,' said Mrs Gordon. 'Keep your eyes on it!'

'Why does she always get to empty the basin?' asked Danny.

'I do not always!'

'You do sot!'

I just took my eyes off the basin for a second – it *was* only a second, honestly it was – and it was all Danny's fault, anyway. If he hadn't distracted me I wouldn't have looked round. The basin wobbled, I tried to right it, and then the whole thing went over. Like a waterfall. And I just *happened* to be passing the long table where we'd been laying out our

magazine entries. I heard the water hit the table. Of
all the luck! McCree luck, my dad would call it.

The whole lot of them were up on their feet
screaming at me. They'd gone berserk. I thought
they were going to kill me. And there was I soaked
to the skin! I could catch pneumonia and die for all
they would care.

'Katy McCree!' they were yelling. 'Now see what
you've done!'

I didn't want to see.

Mrs Gordon ordered them to their seats. Then she
looked at me.

'I told you to keep your eye on it, didn't I, Katy?'

'Yes, Mrs Gordon.' I stared at her feet.

'What are we going to do about our magazine?' wailed Alison. 'She's *ruined* it.'

'It's not totally ruined,' said Mrs Gordon in that very calm voice of hers that sounds as tight as a drum. She picked up four or five sopping pages. Water dripped off them. 'These will have to be done again, obviously. We'll have to work extra hard to repair the damage, that's all.'

All! I wasn't popular for the rest of the day, let me tell you! Alison took me into the house and lent me some of her clothes to put on while mine dried over their Aga cooker. She gave me the oldest jeans she had with a patch on the knee. She didn't speak to me.

'I didn't *mean* to do it,' I said to her back.

'How is it there's always trouble when you're around, Katy McCree?' she inquired, swinging round to face me. She sounded just like a teacher.

I was glad when it was time to go home that afternoon. Will came and sat beside me on the bus. He was grinning. At least one person had forgiven me.

By Friday they'd all got over it, except for Alison, who every now and then got in a little dig. When *she* bumped into me, she called me 'clumsy clot'! 'Clumsy clot yourself!' I told her.

We were setting out the baking on the table for our lunch-time sale when Davie arrived. He was early, we hadn't even heard him toot. He must have driven really fast. He had a grin on his face and an envelope in his right hand which he was waving above his head.

'Give it to us, Davie!' I cried, and jumped for it. I snatched the letter from his hand.

Mairi was chosen to open it since she always stays cool. Like a cucumber. (Who'd want to look like a cucumber?) Annie was so excited she had to run off to the toilet.

'What does it say?' we demanded. 'Read it, Mairi!'

'Dear pupils of Glen Findie Primary School,' Mairi began in her 'important' voice. 'Thank you very much for your letter, which I must say was very nicely written.'

'Skip that bit!' I said. 'That's what my mum would call flannel.'

43

'I have to tell you that I do agree with much of what you say —'

'*Much*,' I groaned.

'Oh, shut up, Katy!' snapped Alison.

'And I do sympathise,' the letter continued, 'but —'

'Here it comes!' I said. 'Here comes the big BUT.'

'Unfortunately the decision does not just rest with me. It is one which has been taken by the members of the Education Committee, to whom I have passed your letter for consideration.'

'It's called passing the buck,' said Davie, pushing his cap back so that he could scratch the top of his bald head.

'I know that, at the moment, you do not want to leave your school in the glen,' the Director's letter carried on, 'but once you did go to the town and made new friends you would find that there were many advantages.'

'We don't want *new* friends,' said Alison.

'We don't want advantages,' said Mary.

'I'm sure it *is* true,' put in Mrs Gordon, 'that it is not just his decision. It's always much more difficult when one has to deal with groups of people called committees. They're faceless, that's the trouble.'

'Whether they've got faces or not,' I said, 'we'll just have to deal with them. We'll have to tell them loud and clear, "HANDS OFF OUR SCHOOL!"'

FIVE

GLEN FINDIE IN REVOLT

Mrs MacDonald held her meeting in the village hall at eight o'clock on Friday evening. I went along with my dad. My mum stayed at home with the younger kids.

'Now mind what you say, Patrick!' my mum warned my dad before we set out.

I enjoyed the three-mile drive down to the village. I like going out on dark evenings. The rain had stopped and the sky was clear. You could see the stars. I picked out the Plough looking like a frying-pan as plain as plain. My dad sang, 'I'm a rambler, I'm a gambler, I'm a long way from home.'

Will and Mairi came with both of their parents, as did Blackberry, though she fell asleep half-way through. Goodness knows how she did with all the noise that went on!

Mairi had brought her tape recorder with her so that she could record the proceedings. That was how she put it. She likes to use words like 'proceedings'. She was going to write the meeting up for the magazine. She said she'd let me listen to the tape too, as I wanted to put some of it into my story as well.

The hall was packed. Parents past and present came, as well as people like Davie who don't have any children themselves. An extra bench was brought in and Mairi and I had to share a chair. I told her she was taking up more than half of it and she told me that she needed more than half as she had to hold the tape recorder. She's got an answer for everything. I ended up standing at the side, which suited me as it gave me a better view.

They were all furious about the Education Committee's decision.

'Scandalous!' declared Mr Johnson.

'Outrageous!' said Mrs McPherson.

'I could use stronger words than that!' cried my dad, jumping to his feet, forgetting my mum's warning.

They went on like that for ages, jumping up and down and shouting. Talk about getting steamed up! Soon the windows had fogged over. Mrs MacDonald had to take off her sheepskin coat and dry her forehead with her hanky. She was having quite a job trying to keep them in order. Even Sam woke up under the table and began to bark and it takes a lot to rouse him. The hall was absolutely seething! It sounded like a wasps' nest.

'The very idea of them trying to take our bairns' school away!' said Mrs Simpson. She's got a soft voice which usually you can't hear behind a bus ticket. Tonight it came booming over the tops of our heads.

'Just let them try it, that's all I say!' That was my dad again. He spent half the evening on his feet with his fists clenched. He's got Irish blood in him. That's what gives him his hot temper, so my mum says.

'They'd take part of our life out of the glen if they did,' said Mrs McPherson.

'Order, order!' shouted Mrs MacDonald, the way the man in the wig does in the House of Commons.

They paid about as much attention to her as the MPs do when he shouts at them. (Have you seen how they carry on in there yelling at one another and roaring with laughter and rolling around on their green benches? At our worst in school we're nowhere near as bad as *that*. Mairi says this is a diversion and to get back to the subject.)

The minister's wife was still calling for order. Her throat was beginning to sound hoarse. She could have done with a throat lozenge or the loan of Mrs Gordon's pointer. After a while she got them calmed down, with the help of Davie, who put two fingers in his mouth and whistled.

'I think a resolution is now called for,' said Mrs MacDonald firmly, letting them know that she was going to stand no more nonsense.

They then drew up the resolution, which meant further arguing and shouting before they could all agree. Some wanted to write screeds, but Mrs Mac-Donald and Mrs Gordon both said that it would be much better to keep the wording strong and simple.

This is what the resolution said:

'We, the inhabitants of Glen Findie, deplore the Education Committee's decision to close our school which has been a focus of community life for more than a hundred years. We are a close and caring community and are deeply shocked by your pro-posal. We strongly urge you to reconsider.'

My dad was muttering about 'urge'. He'd wanted

49

to say 'demand' or 'insist'. Later, he said some of them were lily-livered. He'd no time for pussy-footing around.

Everyone present went up to the table to put their signatures on the piece of paper. Mairi and Will and I were allowed to sign as well. And Blackberry was woken up to print her name. Mrs MacDonald said that she would take the resolution round the glen next day and get every man, woman and child to sign who wanted to sign. That would mean everybody! Who in their *right* mind would want to shut our school?

'Now remember to write to everyone you can think of!' urged the minister. 'The newspapers, our MP —'

'Aye, attack on all fronts!' cried my dad.

Just as we were getting packed up to go home and Mairi and Will and I were stacking the chairs, a reporter and photographer arrived from *The Banner*. That's our weekly county paper. It comes out on a Thursday. They're always looking for bits and pieces of news. If you drop litter in the town's main street you've a good chance of getting your name in the paper.

At the start of the meeting, Mrs MacDonald had said she'd invited *The Banner* to attend and had told them seven-thirty so as to have a sporting chance of them turning up by eight. They're late for everything. They said they'd got held up. (Probably in the pub.)

Anyway, late or not, we were pleased to see them. We were going to need all the publicity we could get. The minister read out the resolution (his wife having lost her voice by this time) and the reporter wrote it down in his notebook.

'So I take it you're not happy about the decision?' he asked, his pencil poised over the page. (What a silly question!)

'Happy?' My dad guffawed. 'We're not going to take this lying down, I can tell you! We're going to fight them every inch of the way.'

The photographer snapped my dad with his fist clenched.

I groaned. Wait till my mum saw this in the paper! She'd do her nut.

We then had our photographs taken, all bunched together, with Mrs Gordon, Mairi, Will, Blackberry and me out in front, and Sam lying across our feet.

'Glen Findie in Revolt,' said the reporter, writing it down so that he wouldn't forget. 'That'll make a good headline.'

SIX

A GLEN SURVEY

I called for Will on Saturday morning – we were going to do another bit of our glen survey. We were investigating different aspects of life in the glen, like how many children in a house, how many pets, how often families went on holiday, where they went, what were the advantages, and disadvantages of each job, et cetera. Then we'd write it up and draw graphs. Some of it would go into the magazine. We were not to ask any questions about money, or anything too personal. (Mrs Gordon was very strict about that!) And we were to check our facts always, not to think that we knew them all. That was what doing surveys was all about.

I'd come down to the farm on my bike but Will's had a puncture and he didn't have any patches to fix it with so we decided to walk. He carried the tape recorder which Mrs Gordon had lent us.

We went first to the village which, as you can see on the map, is about half a mile from the school and is made up of the church and the manse, the village hall, the shop-cum-post office, five cottages and the hotel, the Findie Inn. The hotel doesn't have any stars and it may not be like the ones on the Costa

Brava with swimming pools and stuff like that, but it's homely. They always have a good fire going in the bar. In summer the landlady, Angie McIntosh, rents out the upstairs rooms to tourists. Nobody wants to come here for their holidays in winter. We don't have any skiing in the area – not downhill – though sometimes people come and ski cross-country, through the passes between the hills. Will and I fancy that. We're saving for cross-country skis.

We went into the shop. It sells everything from frozen food to fishing permits and paraffin to postage stamps.

'Come away in,' said Mr McBean, clearing a space on the counter top to lean on between the boxes of jelly babies and liquorice allsorts and piles of newspapers. It was a job to keep him to the subject – shopkeeping – as he wanted to talk about the school closure instead.

'If you ask me, we should have a sit-in at the school,' he said, though we hadn't asked him. He knows a lot about things like 'sit-ins'. Stands to reason he does. He reads more newspapers than anyone else in the glen. He's got loads of free time – he's never exactly run off his feet – and he can read all the papers for free.

Will pressed the record button on the tape recorder. 'Do you enjoy being a shopkeeper, Mr McBean?'

'It's all right.'

All the Primary Ones and Twos want to be shop-keepers when they grow up. Mrs Gordon got them to write out a list of the things they'd keep in their shop. Here are some of the things they put down, in their own words, with their own spelling:

swetes   wurms   lastik bands   bnanas   nales
kloklat   joos   solt and vinegar krisps   bred
lollys   marbels   biskits   ice creem   mato sawce
ryce krispys   bloons

They all plumped for sweets and crisps and ice-cream. Blackberry wrote 'a milyon jars of doly mix-ters' and then tried to draw them but didn't have enough room on the page so the jars got smaller and smaller until they became dots.

'It must be quite nice?' I said. 'Being a shop-keeper? Though I don't suppose you'd ever get rich.'

'Rich? That'd be the day, wouldn't it, Jeanie?' he called across to his wife, who was behind the post office grill with her glasses on counting sheets of stamps. 'Us rich?'

'What are you havering on about now, Donald?' Mrs McBean pulled her glasses down over her nose and frowned over the top of them. When she does that she looks a bit like an owl.

'I said we'll never be rich.'

She snorted at that and pulled the glasses back up and carried on counting stamps.

'Mr McBean, when did you last go on holiday?' asked Will, shoving the tape recorder right under his nose.

'Holiday?' Mr McBean looked as if we'd asked him when he'd last gone to the moon. 'Haven't had a holiday as long as I can remember. Who'd mind the shop?'

'I would,' I offered.

He didn't take me up on it, unfortunately. 'Now if we had a sit-in at the school – occupied it – then we'd get national media coverage. *The Banner*'s all very well but it's hardly going to move them in their corridors of power.'

Corridors of power! I liked that bit. I made a note to ask Mrs Gordon to write it on the blackboard in capital letters.

CORRIDORS OF POWER

'So would you say the disadvantage of keeping a shop means that you can never go on holiday?' Will wasn't going to let him off the hook. It's not easy doing projects in a glen like ours.

'I've never given it a minute's thought.'

Just then the door blew open and in came Mrs MacDonald with her sheepskin coat-tails flying.

'Have you seen Sam?' she gasped. Her face was brick-red.

'Sam?' said I.

'He's gone.'

'Gone?' said Will.

Well, of course neither Will nor I could imagine Sam *going* anywhere.

'I just slipped over to the Findie Inn to have a word with Mrs McIntosh about her veins —'

'Veins?' said I.

'Yes, she's got a bad leg and might have to have an operation. Oh, only a small one. Dr Begg was up seeing her last night. Anyway, I'd left Sam in the kitchen as he was asleep —' (Surprise, surprise!) 'I hadn't shut the back door properly. And when I came home he was gone.'

We went over to the manse with Mrs MacDonald and helped look for Sam. The minister had gone to visit the sick, she said, though she didn't say who they were. She was too het up about Sam. It wasn't like Sam, she kept saying.

The door leading from the kitchen into the hall was shut, and had been all the time, said Mrs MacDonald, so Sam couldn't be in the house. He must have smelled spring in the air, she imagined. Well, she knows Sam better than we do so we didn't argue.

We looked everywhere for him: under the pile of yellowing newspapers on the kitchen floor, in the heap of old cardboard boxes piled up below the window, inside the overflowing garbage bag, in the woodshed, behind the garage, under the scraggly bushes by the gate.

We carried our search over into the churchyard.

Near the gate are the old graves with their stones leaning over and their lettering worn away by wind and rain. Some are Celtic crosses, one or two have skulls and crossbones. We like trying to make out the names and dates on these stones. One says 1689, another 1723. Further back, and round the edges of the yard, are the newer graves where people like old Mrs Lawrie, who died last autumn, aged ninety-two, are buried. Sam was not to be seen skulking behind any of the graves, old or new. We went back into the street.

We asked at all the houses round about. No one had seen Sam. We called his name. The McIntoshes' black labrador lifted his head and howled. It didn't seem like a good omen.

'What could have happened to my poor old Sammy?' moaned Mrs MacDonald.

'I expect he'll come home soon,' said Will.

'He's probably just taking a wee nap somewhere,' said I.

I don't think we convinced Mrs MacDonald. She was still looking right down in the dumps when we left her, after promising to keep our eyes open as we went up the glen. We were due next at the school-house.

'I hope Sam's not rolled over and died some-where,' I said.

We cut sticks and poked the undergrowth as we went, though in winter there aren't too many places where a dog as fat as Sam could hide himself. We called his name every now and then, and whistled.

The Gordons hadn't seen him, either.

'He's getting on, of course.' Mr Gordon shook his head. I supposed he was used to old dogs dying.

We interviewed Mr and Mrs Gordon in their sitting-room. They gave us orange juice and wrapped chocolate biscuits. (Mr McBean had given us an iced lolly each on our way out, which we'd eaten on our Sam-hunt.) The Gordons answered our questions very politely and didn't try to get us off the subject.

Mr Gordon said the advantage of being a vet was that he liked working with animals and he was his own boss. The disadvantage was that he had to get up in the middle of the night when animals were ill or having problems giving birth. But that didn't happen too often.

And what were the advantages and disadvantages of being a teacher? we asked.

Mrs Gordon laughed. She said the good part was that it was great fun and very interesting, which was most of the time. The bad part was that we drive her up the wall at times! We all had a good laugh at that.

'I wouldn't mind being a vet when I grow up,' I said, as Will and I left the schoolhouse and made our way up to the McPhersons' house.

'I think I'd like to be a jet pilot.'

'But not the kind that flies low over the glen!'

Bruce had written an article for the magazine on low-flying jets and how they upset the animals and the people. Sometimes the jets come over so low you think they're going to take the roof off your house. It shouldn't be allowed: that's what we all think. My dad shakes his fist at them but of course they don't pay any attention. They go so fast they probably don't even see him.

'I'll fly long-distance to Australia and China, places like that.'

'But won't you have to be a farmer? What would your dad do?'

Will shrugged. 'Dunno. Don't expect he'd be too pleased.'

'Maybe Mary could be the farmer?'

'Aye, maybe.'

We stopped at the bridge and looked under it, just in *case* Sam might have staggered that far. Though we knew it wasn't likely. There was no sign of him. The brown water was racing madly.

'If he fell in he'd get swept away.' I felt sad. I couldn't get poor old Sam out of my mind. I kept imagining him lying in a ditch, with his eyes closed, for good. Mrs MacDonald would be in an awful state. She hasn't got any children.

'Come on,' said Will, 'I'll race you to the McPhersons' door!'

Meanie! He'd caught me off guard so he got away a couple of seconds before me. We like to race one another. We arrived dead level at the McPhersons', and winded, so that when the door opened I almost fell inward. I had a stitch in my side. Neither of us could speak for the first couple of minutes. Mrs McPherson is a social worker so I expect she's used to people not in full control of themselves.

'Mrs MacDonald's Sam is lost,' I said, when I'd got my breath back.

'Goodness me! Poor Mrs MacDonald. I'll need to go down and see her later.'

Mrs McPherson brought out apple juice and chocolate-backed digestive biscuits and sat us on the floral settee which she had covered herself. She'd made the rag rug in front of the fire, too. She's good at a lot of things, just like Mairi. (Mairi was out with Alison, doing other houses, mine amongst them. I shuddered to think what my dad would be saying into the tape recorder for the whole school to hear afterwards!)

Mrs McPherson spoke for a long time about being a social worker so that we began to worry that the tape would run out. The work was interesting, she said, as well as being varied, challenging, and important. The down side was that it drained your energy and everyone blamed you when anything went wrong.

'Whereas we're only human, you know!'

Social Workers Are Only Human: that's the heading we're going to put on Mrs McPherson's interview.

We went outside to look for Mr McPherson. We found him mucking out the cow byre. He keeps the croft. He doesn't like being inside the house, not when he could be out. He has a cow, twelve hens, two donkeys and twelve goats. (When we listened to the tape later we could hear the cow mooing and a hen squawking and the wind blowing in the background.)

'Why do you like being a crofter, Mr McPherson?' asked Will.

'You're a free man. You don't have to answer to nobody.'

'Not even Mrs McPherson?' I asked.

Will glowered at me. I supposed he thought that came under being too personal. Anyway, Mr McPherson didn't answer my question. Possibly hadn't heard. And he wouldn't tell us any disadvantages.

Crofters Are Free Men: that'll be his heading.

We continued on up to the Smiths, who gave us dandelion coffee to drink instead of juice. It didn't taste of dandelions or coffee. It was sort of tasteless. And we had parsnip cake to eat, which was better than it sounds. (We weren't expecting chocolate biscuits there.)

The Smiths' cottage has white walls inside that

are covered with pictures (some of them a bit funny), and the furniture is stripped pine and the rugs are lovely colours like jewelly greens and pinks and soft purples, and they're handwoven. Mr and Mrs Smith said that to be a painter was a marvellous privilege in life. You might not make much money – they laughed at the very idea – but you were free to express yourself.

'And to live in a wonderful place like this,' said Mr Smith.

'And to be able to send our children to school in a happy environment,' said Mrs Smith.

'Children?' I asked hopefully, latching on at once.

'Oh yes, we plan to have lots more!' said Mrs Smith.

'As a matter of fact there's going to be another one by summer,' said Mr Smith. 'Isn't that right, Blackberry?'

Blackberry was too busy mixing flour (wholemeal) and water for a cake to answer. There was as much flour on her as in the bowl but her mother and father didn't seem to be bothered. It's nice and easy-going in their house. No shouting or arguing. Mrs Smith doesn't believe in raising your voice. A bit quiet though, mind you. There's always a racket going on in our house.

'That's great!' I said. 'Another baby!'

'Yes, we think so, too,' said Mr Smith.

We left, feeling cheered by the news, even though we knew it would be a while before the new Smith would be ready for school.

When we'd gone a bit further up the glen we heard the voices of children playing. Will and I looked at one another. They seemed to be coming from old Mrs Lawrie's house. It had been on the market since she died — Will's uncle was the agent. We broke into a run.

We slowed when the house came into sight. There was a car parked in front of its door, and running round the overgrown garden were *three* children, two boys and a girl.

'All school age too!' said Will.

SEVEN

STRANGERS

We parked our feet on the bottom rung of the gate and leant over.

'Hi!' said I.

'Hello,' said the older of the two boys.

'My name's Katy McCree. This here is Will Johnson. What do they call you?'

'David.' He spoke uncertainly as if he wasn't used to being spoken to by strange children. He glanced backwards towards the house.

Almost immediately, a woman came out of the open door, followed by a man. The parents. The girl, who was younger than the boys, ran to stand by her mother's side.

The woman smiled. She had a bright smile and seemed friendly.

'Hello there! Do you live in the glen?' She took the girl by the hand and brought her over to the gate. The rest of the family followed.

I told them where Will and I lived.

'And do you go to school locally?' asked the father.

'We go to Glen Findie Primary School,' answered Will. 'It's on the other side of the river.'

'We've driven past it. It looks a nice little school?'

'It's great!' I said. 'It really is. Mrs Gordon's our teacher and she's fantastic! She knows about everything under the sun. I'm not kidding – she really does! She could go on *Mastermind*.'

'Do you just have the *one* teacher?' asked the boy, David. He sounded astonished. 'For the whole school?'

'We like that. It's more friendly.'

'We have a visiting music teacher as well,' put in Will. 'She gives us singing and the recorder.'

'There must be *twenty* teachers in our school,' said David. Boasting. I was going off him, fast. Not that I was ever really on.

'Small is beautiful,' I told him. 'That's what Mrs Gordon says.'

'She seems an interesting woman?' said the man.

'Oh, very! So's her husband, Mr Gordon. He's a vet. He helps us do projects on animals. We do a lot of projects. In fact, we're doing one now. We're surveying the glen.'

The woman sighed. 'Sounds idyllic, doesn't it, Paul? Far removed from the false values of the city.'

(It was just as well Will had got the tape recorder switched on. Otherwise we'd never have been able to remember all this. False Values of the City.)

'The school bus comes up both sides of the glen picking up children in the mornings,' said Will. 'It brings us home in the afternoon, too.'

'So the parents don't have to do any ferrying of kids around,' I added, in case the information hadn't sunk in.

The woman looked away from us and over towards the hills which were hidden under a bank of thick, grey cloud that had settled on them since morning. But that didn't seem to bother her. 'It's very beautiful here. You're lucky children.'

I knew we weren't supposed to ask about anything to do with money, but I was going to burst if I didn't ask this particular question.

'Are you thinking of buying?'

The man nodded. 'Yes, we're *thinking.*'

'You'd love it, I tell you you would. And the children would love the school.'

'Oh, the children wouldn't be going to school here,' said the woman.

'No?'

'Oh, no. If we buy it'll be for a holiday house. We both work in Glasgow, you see. We couldn't possibly live here all year round.'

Will and I took off fairly soon after hearing that. We were fed up. I kicked a stone so hard that I stubbed my toe. (I've still got the bruise to show for it.) I was wearing trainers even though my mum had yelled at me to put on my wellies before I went out. But I can't stand wellies unless it's bucketing. They hold me back. I can run faster in soft shoes. And it doesn't bother me if I get my feet a bit damp.

'Holiday house!' I snorted. I felt as if the clouds had settled on top of my head.

There are two or three other holiday houses in the glen and we've got used to the folk. In a way it's quite good having other kids to play with in the summer. It makes a change. But we didn't want Mrs Lawrie's house to go that way as well. It's got an upstairs and is big enough for a family to live in all year round.

'They might *not* buy,' said Will.

'We should have told them the roof has dry rot.'

I wanted to go back and tell them then but Will told me not to be an idiot.

'Couldn't you get your uncle to refuse to sell to them?'

'You're off the wall at times, Katy McCree, really you are!' Will said, so I pushed him – wouldn't you? – and he pushed me, and we both slipped and fell in the mud. We picked ourselves up and glared at one another. We were right looking sights. It was then that we heard a bark.

Will frowned. 'Sounded a bit like Sam.'

That's what I'd thought too. It was a deep, old bark. No young dog had made that noise. It had come from the direction of the house.

'You're right,' I said, forgetting that I'd just decided that I wasn't going to speak to Will. 'Maybe they've kidnapped him.'

'What would anyone want to kidnap Sam for?'

The bark came again.

We retraced our steps back along the path to Mrs Lawrie's house. We heard another bark. A not very happy bark. Definitely not happy.

'It's coming from the outhouse,' said Will.

We crept up to the gate. There was no sign now of the family. Presumably they were inside looking the house over. We opened the gate and sped across the grass to the outhouse.

The bar was in place across the door.

'Sam?' I whispered.

He barked again. He couldn't be as deaf as he made out, or else he sensed our presence.

We unbarred the door, and out he waddled. Hearing footsteps behind us, we whirled around to see the man from Glasgow.

'What did you steal the minister's wife's dog for?' I demanded.

EIGHT

RED FACES

It was all terribly embarrassing. For, of course, they hadn't really stolen Sam. In fact, the dog wasn't even Sam, only his spitting image, being old and a brown and white spaniel. And he had rheumy eyes, too, like Sam, and a fold of loose skin under his mouth.

I wanted to sink into a hole in the ground and disappear from sight, and I could see from the look on Will's face that that was what he wanted me to do, too.

'Meet Horatio!' said the man, holding out his hand towards Sam's double.

Horatio was not in the least bit interested in meeting us, even though we'd set him free. He slouched over to the house, heaved himself up the front step and flopped inside. He moved just *like* Sam. Though their tails were different, I saw: Sam's was longer and brushier.

'We locked Horatio up because we were afraid he might run off,' said the man.

He must have been joking. That dog couldn't have run if a coven of witches' cats had been chasing him.

I tried to say that I was sorry, I hadn't meant it, but I kept spluttering and tripping over the words. Will jumped in and explained about Sam and how we were worried about him.

'Mrs MacDonald is terribly upset, you see —'

'That's OK. I didn't think you'd seriously accuse me of dog theft!' The man was grinning, all over his face. He'd probably tell all his friends back in Glasgow.

'I'm sorry,' I muttered again. The boy, David, was coming out of the house.

'What's up, Dad?' he asked.

Will and I backed away, and as soon as we were out of earshot Will opened up on me. 'What a twit you are, Katy McCree! Why do you *always* have to put your great big foot in it?'

I did not reply. There are times when I wonder why I bother with Will Johnson. I really do.

We arrived at the Ramsays' not speaking. The Ramsays were getting out of their car, which was loaded to the gunnels with boxes and carrier bags. They'd been to Inchbeg on a shopping trip. Bruce and Lynne were helping carry in the loot. Glenda, their wee sister, who'll be coming to school in August, had a huge bagful of sweets which she was clutching with both hands.

'See!' she said, sticking the bag under our noses, then whipping it away quickly.

Bruce staggered past us, his head hidden by a box

filled with enough toilet-rolls to supply the whole glen.

'What have you two been up to then?' asked Mrs Ramsay, eyeing my muddy trousers. She'd been to the hairdresser's and was wearing the fur coat that Mr Ramsay had bought her for Christmas, and her high heels. (My mum can't understand how he manages to pay for all the things. I expect they're bought on the never-never.) Mrs Ramsay is very good, though, at managing the ruts in the road in high heels. She doesn't go over on her ankle as often as you'd think. I tried walking down the road in my mum's party shoes once. The heel snapped off. I won't tell you what she said!

'We're doing our survey of the glen.'

'Oh yes, Bruce was telling us. Mrs Gordon keeps you busy, I will say that!'

'We were wondering if we could interview Mr Ramsay?' He had disappeared inside carrying an enormous box of tins. He'd been buckling at the knees and hadn't had enough puff to do more than nod at us as he went by.

'*Interview* him?'

'About his job.'

'We're doing pieces about all the different jobs people have in the glen,' Will explained. 'Vet, farmer, shepherd, artist —'

'Tinker, tailor,' I said, and laughed. Mrs Ramsay didn't, though. She's not much of a laugher. She's

74

better at frowning, which was what she was doing now. I carried on, 'So we'd like to ask Mr Ramsay about being a road surveyor.'

'I'm sure he doesn't want to talk about *that*,' said Mrs Ramsay in a real sniffy sort of voice. Then she swept past us, carrying two bulging plastic bags in either hand, and went into the house. She kicked the front door shut behind her with the back of a high heel.

'What's up with her?' I wondered. 'We seem to be getting on the wrong side of everybody this after-noon.'

'*We* do?' said Will.

Bruce came back out to collect two boxes of soap powder, both giant size.

'She must do a lot of washing, your mum,' I said.

He shrugged.

'What's up with her?'

Bruce's face turned a beetrooty shade.

'She nearly bit our noses off. We only wanted to ask your dad a few questions about his job.'

Bruce bent over and lifted up the soap boxes, concentrating the way a weight-lifter does.

'Come on, you!' said Will, and caught hold of my arm, just about dislocating it. I let him drag me away. I glanced back at Bruce.

'There's something going on at the Ramsays', Will, that's for sure!'

We re-crossed the bridge, back onto the other side

of the river. Now that we were nearing the village again we kept a fresh look-out for Sam. No sign. No sound. The place was dead quiet. They were probably all sitting in front of the telly watching Saturday Grandstand. (I knew my dad would be, and my mum would be saying, 'I thought you were going to mend that gate this afternoon?')

I suggested that we call in at the manse and see how Mrs MacDonald was doing. She might be in need of cheering up.

We went round the back of the house and chapped on the door.

'Come away in,' she called. 'Door's open.'

It always is. Even at night she usually forgets to lock it. She says they've got nothing worth stealing. Not that there are many thieves going about in our parts. Not like the city. At the thought of stealing and thieves my cheeks turned hot and I remembered the look of amusement on the man from Glasgow's face when I'd accused him of being a thief.

We opened the door.

'We've looked everywhere for Sam, Mrs MacDonald,' I began, then stopped.

She was sitting in a chair beside the Aga cooker, with a brown and white rug lying across her feet. The rug was rising and falling, keeping time with the snores that were coming from it.

'How did *he* get here?' I asked.

'He was in the house the whole time, would you

believe! I must have left the kitchen door open after all! And when he went into the hall the door must have slammed shut behind him. I found him lying on the settee in the sitting-room, fast asleep. Naughty boy, aren't you, Sammy, you old rascal?' She reached down and gave the rug a tickle. 'He knows he's not allowed on the settee.'

He opened one eye. I could have sworn that if he'd had the energy, he'd have winked.

NINE

THE RAMSAYS DROP
A BOMBSHELL

We were soon to find out what was up with Mrs
Ramsay. Bruce came into school on the Monday
morning looking as if someone had pinched his scone.
He didn't say much, though we didn't think anything of that since he never does say much. But he
didn't join in our game of football, either. He
trudged on into school without lifting his head.
When we came in he was sitting at his desk colouring
in his project on rocks. He's keen on rocks – agates,
cairngorms, quartzes, and the like. He has quite a
big collection at home. He still didn't look up.

We started off the day with Will and me bringing
the others up to date with our part of the glen
survey.

'We didn't get to interview Bruce's dad,' I said.
'His mum didn't seem to think he'd want to talk
about being a road surveyor.' I looked over at
Bruce, who was carrying on colouring in as if he
hadn't heard. But I thought he had. The edges of
his ears were petunia-pink.

'Our daddy's getting a new job,' announced
Lynne, dropping the Ramsays' bombshell for them

right into the middle of the classroom.

'A *new* job?' said I.

Lynne nodded importantly. 'In Glasgow.'

'*Glasgow!*'

We were stunned, as if someone had swiped us with sandbags. Bruce's face had taken on that beetroot shade again, all over.

'He might not be getting it,' he muttered. 'We don't know yet.'

'Mummy thinks they'll call him down to Glasgow next week.' Lynne's more chattery, the way her mother usually is.

'He's waiting to hear if he's got an interview,' said Bruce, then he added vehemently (for him, at any rate), '*I* don't want to go to Glasgow.' And he lifted his head and looked at the teacher.

'I don't suppose you do, Bruce,' she said. 'But you have to go where your father's − or mother's − work takes you.'

Only about half of our mothers work − outside the home, that is. Mrs Gordon jumps on us if we say that the mothers at home don't work. It's hard work being a mother, she says. And it's more difficult for women to get paid work in country districts than the cities. They don't have a lot of choice.

'Our mummy wants to go to Glasgow,' said Lynne.

We knew that Mrs Ramsay would. That was where she lived before she married Mr Ramsay. She met him at a ceilidh in the village hall when she came up for her holidays one summer. She stayed in a caravan on the Johnsons' farm. She says that if she'd come in winter she'd have gone back down to Glasgow as if she had skates on her feet. She likes bright lights and shops. Big, bustly shops, with different departments and strip lighting. Not wee shops like the McBeans' which has dangling light bulbs and no shades and keeps itself warm (sort of) with a smelly paraffin heater. And she hates the long dark winter nights. Like now. Dark by half-past three. She says you might as well be living in Siberia.

Now Mr Ramsay is a real glen man. He likes fishing and bird-watching. He wouldn't be able to do much of that in Glasgow. He doesn't care about street lights and department stores. We supposed that Mrs Ramsay must have talked him into applying for the job.

'Mummy will be able to get a job in Glasgow,' Lynne went on. She was enjoying being the centre of attention. 'And then we'd have more money coming in and we could go on *two* holidays a year. Mummy wants to go to Gran Canaria. Our Aunty Betty went to Gran Canaria last year. We went to Lanzarote.'

Mairi then put into words what we were all thinking. '*If* Mr Ramsay gets the job, and they move to Glasgow, the school roll will be down to *twelve*.'

'And Glenda wouldn't be coming in August,' said

81

Mary.

'They'll shut us for sure now!' I declared. 'That settles it!'

'I'm sorry.' Bruce sounded miserable.

'You're not to feel badly, Bruce,' Mrs Gordon said quickly. 'It's not your decision. Nor can we expect your father to pass up the chance of a good job just to keep our roll up. Now then, children, get your sums jotters out. It's time we got down to work.'

She was in a brisk mood for the rest of the morning; wouldn't let us have any chat at all. But at break-time she couldn't stop our mouths. Mr Ramsay's job was the only thing we could talk about.

'He might not get it,' Bruce kept saying.

'He might, though,' I said. 'He probably will. He's not stupid your dad, is he? And then what? We'll get bussed in to Inchbeg. We'll have to leave every morning in the dark in winter-time. And we won't get back till dark at night. It'd be awful for our Annie and the other Wee Ones. It'd make a really long day for them.'

'Lay off Bruce!' said Alison.

'I'm not *on* him!'

'Yes, you are, Katy McCree! You keep going on.'

'What about yourself, Alison Gordon? Are you trying to kid on you don't care? If they do shut the school your mother'll be out of a job. *And* a house.

They'll put you out. They'll sell the house and the
school to get the money. You might have to live in a
caravan.'

Mairi stepped between us.

When we went back into school, Mrs Gordon said, 'Now, children, we must all stay calm. When there's a crisis people's tempers tend to get short and their feathers ruffled. But falling out and squabbling won't help the situation at all. Quite the reverse!'

She gave Alison and me her special stern look. She'd probably been watching out of the window.

'Anyway,' she went on, 'perhaps the Education Committee will listen to what we're saying and change its mind.'

'But if they thought a roll of fourteen was bad, what'll they make of twelve?' I asked.

We were on edge again now whenever Davie the Post was due. Would he have brought a letter from Glasgow for Mr Ramsay? I tried quizzing Davie, but he just grinned and shook his head and said he wasn't allowed to divulge the secrets of Her Majesty's Mail.

'I was only asking if there *was* a letter. Not what was in it.'

'I should hope not indeed! How would I know what was in anybody's letter?'

(He knows what's on postcards, mind you. He'll tell you if the Ramsays or the Smiths are having good weather on their holiday. But you'd need to be a saint not to read postcards, wouldn't you? And nobody ever writes anything important on them, anyway.)

Mrs Ramsay told Mrs McPherson that she was hopeful. She thought that her husband had a good chance of getting the job. He was well qualified. The post he'd applied for was in the Roads Department of Strathclyde Regional Council, and it was a better job than he had here. Mrs Ramsay thought it was time her husband started going for promotion.

'She wants him to get his foot on the ladder,' reported Lynne.

It was a long week. On Thursday *The Banner* came out, and there we all were on the front page, my dad with his clenched fist in the air! GLEN FINDIE IN REVOLT, said the headline.

'It's good coverage,' said Mrs Gordon, cutting it out to stick on the noticeboard.

My mum was less pleased. She asked my dad how was it that *he* always managed to draw attention to himself in the wrong way?

On Friday, the letter arrived for Mr Ramsay. Bruce told us that it had when he came back after lunch. Will and I had been hanging around the bridge waiting for him.

'The minute I saw it I knew. It was official-looking. Dad wasn't in but he'd said for Mum to open it.'

'He's got an interview?' I held my breath.

'Next Friday. At eleven.'

TEN

DEADLINES

Two deadlines loomed ahead: the entry date for *The Scotsman*'s School Magazine competition and Mr Ramsay's interview in Glasgow. They would both fall on the same day: next Friday.

I didn't like the sound of dead lines. When I asked Mrs Gordon why they were called that she said we should look it up in the dictionary. (Maybe she didn't know herself.) So we looked it up and saw that it meant a line drawn round a military prison. If a prisoner stepped over it he was shot.

'What if your foot slipped?' said Danny.

'That wouldn't happen nowadays,' said Mrs Gordon. 'Today we are more civilised.'

CIVILISED: she wrote it on the blackboard and we copied it into our jotters.

'What does that mean?' asked Lynne.

'Nice and kind.' Mrs Gordon spoke briskly now, to let us know that she wanted no more chat and we should get on with our work.

On Saturday, the Ramsays went to town again. They had a busy morning. Mrs Ramsay bought Mr Ramsay a new shirt and a new tie. She put his suit into the cleaner's. Then she took him to the hairdresser's to get his hair cut.

We learned all this on Monday morning, when Lynne wrote it up in her News Book.

The shirt was blue-and-white striped, the tie Paisley-patterned, in blue and red. Mrs Ramsay had wanted Mr Ramsay to get a new suit as well.

'But he drew the line at that,' said Lynne.

'A dead line?' asked Danny. 'Bang, bang, you're dead!' He clutched his chest.

'That'll do, Danny!' said Mrs Gordon.

Lynne carried on, 'My dad said what if he didn't get the job?'

We could see Mr Ramsay's point. He already had a suit for weddings and funerals, and for going to the Christmas Dance at the County Hotel in the town.

'Mummy bought scuff polish for his shoes too,' added Lynne.

Bruce was muttering under his breath. I could sympathise. That's the only trouble with having younger sisters and brothers in the same classroom: they can give you a red face.

Our Annie was writing up our family's news: that our mum had given our dad a row for getting his picture in *The Banner* with his fist clenched. Fortunately Annie's spelling is so bad that no one knew what she was writing except me. Danny was continuing his long-running serial about the good fairy and the witch. At present they were hanging over a cliff backwards.

In my News Book, I wrote, 'Friday is looming ahead of us like a great big black cloud. When eleven strikes the cloud will open and the rain will fall on our heads in plummets.'

'You can't use plummets like that,' Mairi objected.

'I'm *using* it!'

Mairi appealed to the teacher. 'It should be used as a verb, shouldn't it, Mrs Gordon? Not a noun?'

'It's usually a verb. Why not look it up in the dictionary?'

Mairi did the looking. She can't keep her hands off the dictionary. 'It *can* be used as a noun.' She sounded disappointed. 'But it means a leaden weight. Rain can't be a *leaden* weight.'

'Yes, it can!' I cried.

'I think,' Mrs Gordon intervened, 'that this can be allowed under "poetic licence".' She'd explained to us the week before that poets can turn words around in their own way to get the effect they want.

'But Katy's not a poet.' Mairi wouldn't give up.

'I write poetry, don't I, Mrs Gordon?'

'You all do.'

I wrinkled my nose at Mairi. So there! 'Anyway,' I said, 'when Mr Ramsay gets the job on Friday the news will *feel* like a leaden weight!'

Then Mairi had to say that no one could be *certain* that Mr Ramsay *would* get the job.

'He probably won't hear on Friday,' put in Bruce. 'Not straight away. They usually write afterwards. At least that's what my dad thinks.'

I groaned. 'Do you mean the agony's going to go on for several more days?'

'I suggest you get on with your work, Katy,' said Mrs Gordon. 'And stop looking so tragic.'

'She thinks she's Mary Queen of Scots about to get her head chopped off,' said Danny. 'Is it true, Mrs Gordon, that people's bodies go on twitching after they lose their heads?'

Mrs Gordon ignored him. Quite right too. 'We've got a lot to do to get the magazine finished this week and off to Edinburgh. How many of the Sixes and Sevens can stay after school to help? We'll need all hands on deck.'

We five Big Ones put our hands up. Blackberry put hers up as well.

'You're not a Six or a Seven,' Alison told her. 'You're a One.'

'I want to be a Six.'

'You will be one day,' said Mrs Gordon.

Blackberry wrote a poem for the magazine.

'I wont to be a SIX
A BIG BIG SIX
And do lots of TRIX
Then I woent be A ONE
And I ill get more fun.'

Alison was making up a crossword for the

magazine with Mairi, and Jamie was doing a riddles page. He loves riddles.

Things like:

My first is in JAM

My second is in KNEE

My third is in TREE

I'm small and creepy. What am I?

'Jamie McCree!' I told him, and he wanted to biff me but he couldn't reach.

After school we Big Ones stayed behind. The lights were on in the classroom. Outside, it was dead dark and the wind was making a waily noise down the chimney. Mrs Scott came in and swept round us, though Mrs Gordon told her not to bother too much. We would tidy up ourselves. Mrs Scott is always shaking her head about the mess we make. In her day they weren't allowed to spill paint on the floor or get plasticine stuck in the grooves of their desks. In her day they didn't do projects. They sat up straight, learned their tables, and had tests every Friday morning.

We worked for two and a half hours. We put some of the material on to the school computer, the rest was to be kept in the pupils' own handwriting. Mrs Gordon thought that looked more interesting, especially when we'd done drawings too. Will and Mairi worked on the lay-out, deciding what items to put together on which page. Alison's design had been chosen for the cover, but not because she's Mrs

Gordon's daughter. The whole school had voted on it. Alison's brilliant at art, I'll give her that. Her drawing shows the school from the road, with the hill behind, and a golden eagle flying over the top of the roof.

At six, Mrs Gordon said we must go home, although we'd have liked to have stayed longer. She had promised our parents that we would leave at six. Mrs McPherson came to pick up Mairi on her way home from work. She was to take Bruce as well. She thought the magazine was looking great.

'It gets better and better, Mrs Gordon, it really does. Surely no one in their right minds would close a school that can produce work like this!'

'Some of them might not be in their right minds,' I suggested.

Mrs McPherson told us that she had written ten letters, to MPs of every political party, to newspapers, to everyone she could think of who might be influential.

'That's what we have to do. Go for the people who have influence!'

She put Mairi and Bruce into the back of her car and drove off.

I was to walk with Will as far as the farm where my dad would meet me.

'Hang on a moment, you two,' said Mrs Gordon, 'and I'll get Mr Gordon to walk you up the road.'

'We're all right,' I protested. 'Will's got a torch. And we're not afraid of the dark, are we, Will?'

'Maybe not.' Mrs Gordon was not going to listen. 'But it is *my* responsibility to make sure you get home safely.' She sent to call her husband, who came, pulling on his jacket and whistling up Jemima. He had a storm lamp with him.

'Right then, kids!'

We set off up the glen, with the lamp sending its beam out in front of us making the frost glitter on the road like diamonds. You almost felt you could snatch them up and hold them in your hands.

The winking diamonds seemed to excite Jemima. She trotted along in front of us, nosing the ground and giving off little frisky barks every now and then. She's quite a young dog. 'A bit skittish yet,' said Mr Gordon. The opposite to Mrs MacDonald's Sam.

Suddenly Jemima stopped and raised her head. She seemed to hear something that we didn't hear for in the next second she was off like a streak, back down the glen. The dark swallowed her up.

'Jemima! Come back, Jemima!' called Mr Gordon, but she didn't come.

'We'll be all right now,' said Will. 'I've got my torch.' He clicked it on. 'We're nearly there.'

'Are you sure?'

Quite sure, we assured him. We had hardly any distance at all to go now to Will's road-end.

'Well, OK then. I'd better get after Jemima, she's acting a bit daft these days. Take care!' Mr Gordon then disappeared into the darkness himself.

'If we have to go to school in town no one'll bother about us the way Mr and Mrs Gordon do,' I said, as Will and I continued up the road. 'We could get eaten by wolves for all they'll care.'

'I don't suppose they'll be *that* bad. Helen says secondary school is great.' (Helen is Will's cousin, the estate agent's daughter.)

'Don't tell me you're changing your mind – about keeping our school open! Just because you're going to secondary in August, Will Johnson!'

'Don't be such a twit, McCree!'

I gave him a shove – he was asking for it! – and he dropped the torch. Clumsy clot! It was only a small shove. The torch landed on the hard road with a crack and the light went out. When Will picked it up he found it wouldn't go on again.

'Now look what you've done!'

'It was you that dropped it! Anyway, we can manage fine without a light. I could find my way home blindfold.'

Well, you might know I shouldn't have said that. Just then the first few flakes of snow came drifting innocently down from the sky. They looked perfectly harmless. I turned up my face and felt the softness of them as they landed on my cheeks. It hadn't snowed much yet this winter and the school had been closed for only one afternoon because of weather.

'I love snow, don't you, Will?'

'We might be able to go tobogganing on the hill.'

'They might even have to shut the school for a few days.'

'But what about the magazine? We can't be late with that.'

'I hope it doesn't snow too much, then. Just a bit. Just enough. To go sledging.'

As I spoke, the snow seemed to thicken. It was as if somebody up there had heard me and wanted to argue back so they'd cranked a handle and sent down a proper flurry. In the next instant, it was thick and blinding. I birled round.

'Where are you, Will?' I cried. '*Will?*'

'Here!'

He grabbed my hand. The wind had strengthened, too, quite suddenly. Where does the wind come from when it gathers up strength like that? One minute it wasn't there, and the next, it was howling like a banshee and driving the snow straight into our faces. We were gasping for breath. There was nothing to see but the twirling, dancing snow: the glen had vanished.

Nobody would have thought, until then, that you could get lost between the school and the Johnsons' farm.

ELEVEN

STORMBOUND

Will and I had strayed off the road. Easy enough to do in a snowstorm. We knew that we must have left it because we could feel the ground soggy underfoot. We were on grass. Clumps of heather clutched at our ankles. And then I fell down a hole!

It must have been a rabbit hole – the place is riddled with them. And I didn't fall right down it but I got my foot caught and went full length on my face. I lay there, my nose in wet heather. I didn't want to get up. I was winded and I didn't like the way my right ankle felt. It might be nice and warm down there in the burrow, I thought. I expected the rabbits would all be asleep. Lucky rabbits! Will hauled me up.

But when I tried to put my right foot to the ground my ankle wobbled and went over. Pain streaked up my leg. Will grabbed me before I went sprawling again.

'It's my ankle,' I moaned. I could hear myself moaning even though the wind was making more noise than I was. My ankle felt as if it was on fire.

Will seemed to catch on to what was wrong. 'Lean on me,' he yelled into my ear. 'You *can't* sit down. You *mustn't* sit down.' He must have guessed that that was exactly what I felt like doing.

He put his arm round my waist (he had to, or I'd have gone over) and I let him take some of my weight. (I had to do that, too − I couldn't take all my own weight, not on that ankle. So you can just stop smirking, Alison Gordon!)

The snow seemed to be getting thicker every second. We stumbled on. I let my good foot watch out for further rabbit holes and when I felt the ground dip I went extra carefully. I didn't fancy doing the second ankle in. We didn't talk. We needed all our energy just to keep going. The wind would have ripped the voices out of our mouths, anyway, if we'd tried to speak. It was coming from the north-west and sweeping the snow in front of it. Soon it would pile up against walls and on roadsides. And then it would drift. That's when the trouble starts. That's when people get really seriously lost.

We knew we mustn't stop, or we could end up frozen stiff. Like corpses. I shivered. But keeping going wouldn't necessarily get us anywhere. We could easily be wandering round in circles. What if we had to spend the night out here on open moorland? The chances were, if we did, that we wouldn't last until morning.

We floundered about for what seemed like hours, but it might have been only twenty or thirty minutes. There was no way you could tell how much time was passing.

Then Will shouted into my ear again. 'The wood! I think we're at the wood!'

We'd blundered into the edge of it. We felt twigs crackling beneath our feet. We put out our hands and touched the spiky branches of the trees. We could just make out their dark tangled shapes with the white snowflakes dancing in amongst them. They looked like really old men and women holding out their arms to us.

We went a little way into the wood, ducking our heads to avoid low-hanging branches. It seemed suddenly quiet in here, although overhead the wind was still howling like a maniac. I felt exhausted, could hardly get my legs to move, one after the other.

After a little while we found a mossy knoll underneath an old Scotch pine. We sat down and, huddling together, leant our backs against the trunk. Babes in the wood! Not that we were babes. And I didn't think it had snowed on them. I tried to remember if anyone had found them. Hadn't the birds covered them with leaves? But there were no birds now. And no leaves. I wondered what my dad would be doing. He'd have known by then that something must have happened to us.

My dad had left for the Johnsons' just after six. My mum had kept telling him to hurry on, I'd be waiting, and the Johnsons would be wanting to have their tea. He was just going, he kept saying. Finally he went, taking Danny with him.

(Danny told me the whole story afterwards.)

They drove down the bumpy track from our place on to the main glen road, which is no motorway, you understand, but only a single track which has its ups and downs and has been patched here and there with splodges of tar macadam. They drove in our old four-wheeled drive Land Rover. It's a bit rickety but it gets there. Most of the time. This time it didn't. It conked out half-way up the Johnsons' track. It spun around as my dad tried to urge it on and ended up slewed sideways.

He had a few unpleasant things to say about the car when he got out. He kicked one of the tyres but that didn't make any difference to it. It just sat there. And then the snow started. That was all they needed!

'Come on,' my dad said to Danny, 'we'll need to hoof it.'

So they hoofed it up to the farmhouse and it was just as well that the lights were shining from the windows or they might have lost their way themselves. When they reached the Johnsons' door they looked like snowmen.

Mrs Johnson brought them into the kitchen and sat them down by the Rayburn stove. Mr Johnson put a wee dram into my dad's hand.

'That'll warm you up, Patrick,' he said.

'Where's our Katy then?' asked my dad, after he'd warmed up.

'They're not back yet,' said Mrs Johnson, who was looking anxious. 'It's half six – they should have been here by now. It doesn't take more than fifteen minutes to walk from the school.'

'Stop worrying, woman!' said Mr Johnson, giving my dad and himself another wee tot to warm up on. 'Women are aye worrying about their bairns! Isn't that right, Patrick?'

'Aye, that's right, Calum. Mine's the same. If she'd nothing to worry about she'd invent it – that's what I tell her.'

'Still, with five children, there always will be something,' said Mrs Johnson, and her voice was quite sharp. She was standing by the window watching the swirling snow. 'It's coming down quite hard, Calum.'

'Will'd know his way home in a pea-soup fog. And he's a strong lad. But if you're bothered, away and ring Mrs Gordon. She's kept them late more than likely. Maybe Mr Gordon'll be bringing them up himself.'

Mrs Johnson rang the schoolhouse and was told that Will and I had left at six prompt, with Mr Gordon. She explained that Jemima had run away and he'd had to go after her.

'But he said they were nearly home. Otherwise he wouldn't have left them.'

It was now a quarter to seven.

'They'll be fooling around in the snow if I know them,' said my dad. But he put down his glass and went to look out of the back door. 'It's a real white-out right enough,' he muttered. 'I think we'd better take a turn down the road, Calum.'

The two men and Danny (who refused to be left behind) took big black rubber torches and went out. They kept close together, putting Danny in the middle. The snow was coming down fast and furious.

They walked down the Johnsons' track, passing our old Land Rover, which was looking like a white ghost, and found the glen road. It wasn't so easy finding it, as Mr Johnson remarked.

When they were part way down the road, they saw another light bobbing about ahead of them.

'It must be them!' shouted my dad.

But it was not. As the light came nearer they saw that it was Mr Gordon with his storm lamp on his way up. That was when they realised that Will and I must be lost.

I could feel myself getting colder and colder and sleepier and sleepier. I kept thinking that maybe we should get up and wave our arms about and stamp our feet. Not that I *could* have stamped my feet, especially my right one! I didn't think I'd even have enough strength left to stand up.

I must have dozed off at some point for my head jerked up and I couldn't think where I was. Then I heard voices.

'Katy! Will!' They were calling. They sounded like ghost voices. Perhaps it was the trees calling, I thought. The old men and women. People who used to live in the glen, a long time ago. Perhaps they'd been evicted during the Highland Clearances and their spirits still haunted the wood.

Will was struggling to sit up beside me.

The voices were coming gradually nearer. They

were still calling our names. Our names were drawn out as they went floating away on the wind. *Wiiiiiill! Kateeeeee!*

'Katy!' Will was saying my name too and shaking me. I couldn't seem to come properly awake.

Then we saw a light. Jumping about amongst the twisted trees.

'Here!' shouted Will. 'We're here!'

Heeeeere ... heeeeere ...

I was amazed that he could still shout. When I tried to, no sound came out of my mouth. (So, OK, it takes a lot to keep me quiet!)

Feet came crashing through the undergrowth, and a whole battery of torchbeams struck us full in the face.

TWELVE

FRIDAY AT ELEVEN

'It's dangerous once you start falling asleep like that,' I said.

That was true, Mrs Gordon agreed.

'We could have died of hypothermia.' It was my mother who'd told me that. She hadn't been too thrilled by the whole affair, as you might imagine. 'Another five minutes and we'd have been gonners.'

'I hope not, Katy!' said Mrs Gordon. Apparently, she and her husband had been in an awful state while we were missing. He'd blamed himself for going after Jemima and not staying with us. But no one could really blame him for we had been only yards from Will's road-end.

I had my ankle, which was wrapped in a crinkly bandage, propped up on a chair. I'd sprained it. I'd had to go down to Dr Begg's surgery in town to have it X-rayed and make sure it wasn't broken. It was quite nice being laid up as everybody had to wait on me, hand and foot. Hand *and* foot! Get that!

Mrs Gordon wrote HYPOTHERMIA on the blackboard. She then gave us a long talk on the perils of bad weather and how careful you had to be, especially in winter. But even in summer, conditions can change quickly in the glen. Sometimes hill walkers get lost when a mist comes down and if they don't have the right clothes on the heat of their bodies starts to ebb away. That's when they get hypothermia. We had to write an essay about it and Mrs Gordon said that Will's should go into the magazine.

We were running a bit behind with the magazine. We'd lost a whole day because of the snow. The school was shut on Tuesday. So, on Wednesday, after school, the Sixes and Sevens stayed on again.

But nobody would be allowed to go home on their own this afternoon. Not even three steps up the road! declared Mrs Gordon. We were still having light falls of snow, but the snow plough was going up the glen twice a day keeping the road clear.

I'd been hoping for even more snow. Enough to block the main road south. So that Bruce's dad wouldn't be able to make it to Glasgow on Friday for eleven.

'They'd just tell him to come next week,' said Mairi.

'How do you know?'

'They wouldn't *not* give him the job just because he'd been snowed in.'

At six o'clock, Mrs Gordon said we'd have to stop even though there was still a great deal to do. We were tired, and couldn't deny it. We were all yawning.

'But it should go off tomorrow, shouldn't it?' asked Mairi anxiously. 'To reach Edinburgh by Friday?'

Mrs Gordon thought *The Scotsman* wouldn't be *so* rigorous about the closing date. She said she would ring them up and tell them that our entry had been delayed by the weather and should arrive by Monday.

'I'm sure they will appreciate that country schools are different.'

Thursday brought one piece of good news. Will came in with it in the morning. His uncle – the estate agent – had not sold Mrs Lawrie's house to the family from Glasgow who'd been going to use it as a holiday house.

'Maybe it was Katy who put them off,' sniggered my nasty little brother Danny. 'When she accused them of stealing Sam.'

So Will had told! Wait till I got hold of him! Then I remembered my ankle and realised I was going to have a job getting hold of anyone for a while.

'Somebody else might buy Mrs Lawrie's house now,' I said to Mrs Gordon. 'Somebody with children. That'd help get the roll up.'

'I think waiting for that is a bit like whistling in the dark, Katy! We'll just have to keep up the fight ourselves.'

Once we got the magazine away we were going to

send off some more letters. Mrs MacDonald had suggested writing to people in the media. Personalities. Pop stars. TV presenters.

A letter from Mrs McPherson had appeared in the *Herald*. Mrs Gordon cut it out and pinned it on the noticeboard beside the cutting from *The Banner*.

'One-teacher School Threatened with Closure,' said the heading in the *Herald*. Mrs McPherson had written a good long letter, four paragraphs in all. It was stirring stuff. She said we were fighting for our way of life. More was at stake than the simple shutting of a school.

'Our glens have had the life-blood drained from them before, starting with the Highland Clearances.'

'That's a good bit,' said Danny, 'about the life-blood.'

We'd done a big project on the Highland Clearances and coloured in on a map the glens of Scotland that had suffered during them. You can see the ruined cottages further up our own glen. In the eighteenth and nineteenth centuries the landlords of the big estates put the crofters out of their homes and leased their land to sheep-farmers from the south. Just so as they could make more money. Money's at the bottom of most things, says my dad. Too much of it, or too little.

'Closing rural schools is another way of clearing our glens,' Mrs McPherson had written.

Dreaded Friday arrived. Everyone's eyes turned to Bruce when he came in in the morning. His father had gone off to Glasgow the afternoon before, dressed in his dry-cleaned suit, his new striped shirt and his Paisley-pattern tie, and with his shoes shining.

'My mum said he looked braw,' reported Lynne.

And he'd arrived. Nothing had happened to him on the way. Unfortunately. I hadn't wanted anything bad to happen to him, but if he could have got stuck in a snowdrift or something like that, it would have been a help.

But he hadn't. His car hadn't even had a puncture. He was in Glasgow, staying with Mrs Ramsay's sister. He'd phoned home to say so.

We put the last touches to the magazine. It was looking good, especially with the four pages of colour photographs. The colour did make a difference. It seemed to bring the magazine to life. Mrs Gordon was pleased with us.

'You've worked hard, children. And regardless of whether we win or not, I'm proud of you. Winning isn't really important, anyway. We've enjoyed doing it, and that is the main thing.'

'I'd still like to win though,' said Danny.

Mrs Gordon put the magazine into a big fawn envelope with a covering letter to say that it was all our own work. It was now ready for Davie.

At eleven, we all looked up at the clock and thought of Mr Ramsay waiting to be called into the interview room.

'I expect he's standing in a Corridor of Power,' said Danny.

Those who went home for lunch went. Will and I walked down to the bridge after we'd eaten our sandwiches. I hirpled, rather. Using a stout stick to lean on that Will had cut for me. The day was bitter cold. Our breath made white puffs in the air. We watched the road leading to the Ramsays' house.

Bruce didn't appear until the lunch-hour was over. We had just heard the tinkle of Mrs Gordon's hand bell when Will caught sight of him.

'Here he comes!'

I turned. Bruce was approaching the bridge from the other side. He had his hands in his pockets and his head was down. He was watching a small stone

that he was dribbling between his feet. The sight of
him made my heart plummet into my boots.

'Don't tell me they offered your dad the job!' I
cried.

'Aye, they did.' Bruce lifted his head. 'On the
spot.'

THIRTEEN

SNAKES AND LADDERS

'I'm very pleased for your father, Bruce,' said Mrs Gordon, sounding far too cheery. Though you could see she didn't feel cheerful underneath. Her eyes had a kind of hazy, slightly faraway look about them. Perhaps she was imagining a furniture van arriving outside her house to take their furniture away. 'I'm sure we all are. It would be very mean of us not to be.'

And she fixed us with a look which said we were not to take it out on Bruce. She'd already jumped on me when I'd come in with the news. All I'd said was, 'He's got the job – we're done for!'

Lynne had started to cry and even though Mrs Gordon had told her (in a kindly voice) that there was nothing to cry about she'd gone on sniffling for the rest of the afternoon. Bruce didn't say a word. He just went on colouring in his agates. He must have done some two or three times over.

'I think you've all got projects to finish,' said Mrs Gordon. 'So get busy!'

'I don't suppose they'll get many projects to do in Glasgow,' I said, as I got out my folder. I was doing a project on vets. Mr Gordon had taken me out with him on his rounds one day. 'They'll probably get sums all day long.'

'Katy, I think you have a distorted idea of what city schools are like. I'm sure they'll do lots of interesting projects.'

'My cousin's at school in Glasgow. There's over thirty in her class, and they have discipline problems. Her teacher had a nervous breakdown last year.'

'If your cousin's got a tongue like yours then I'm not surprised!'

Ha, ha. Very funny, I must say. Everyone laughed. Except me.

School was closing early that day. Mrs Gordon had to go to a meeting. Mrs Ramsay came down in her car to pick up Bruce and Lynne. She was dressed to kill, as my Auntie Jean would say. High-heel shoes, dangly earrings, chunky bracelets – the lot! And she was smiling, all over her face. They were going to town, she said. To celebrate, I supposed.

'We're going to have burgers and Coke,' announced Lynne. 'Double cheeseburgers with chips.'

'I want a double burger,' said Annie, as we stood waiting for Mungo the Bus.

'Well, you can't have it,' I snapped. I could feel my own mouth watering at the thought of a double cheeseburger. With a big mountain of chips. Sizzling hot, and loads of salt and vinegar and tomato sauce.

'I want one,' Annie went on wailing.

I limped up to the back of the bus, well away

111

from the younger members of my family. I was
finding my ankle a problem when I wanted to get
away from Annie and Florrie.

'You're lucky you've only got one sister,' I told
Will. 'And no brothers.'

'Want to get off with me?' he asked. 'Floss has just
had some new pups, born last night.'

So I got off with him, which enraged Annie and
Jamie, who wanted to see the new puppies too. I
waved to them as the bus disappeared up the road.

Mrs Johnson gave us tea and warm scones straight
out of the oven. They helped make up for the
burgers. We spread them with butter and thick
homemade raspberry jam.

'Fabulous!' I cried.

We told Will's mum about Mr Ramsay's job.

'It's all Mrs Ramsay's fault.'

'I don't think we should blame her like that,
Katy,' said Mrs Johnson.

'No?'

'Well, look at it from her point of view. She misses
her family in Glasgow, and life in the glen doesn't
really suit her. Yet she's lived here for the last twelve
years. Maybe it was time that Mr Ramsay started to
consider her.'

I wasn't sure that I liked the sound of all this.
Mairi's mother had said to her, 'Mrs Ramsay has
needs too, you know,'

What was going on? Suddenly all the mothers

seemed to be taking Mrs Ramsay's side, even though they didn't want the school roll to drop. Nothing was ever straightforward, it seemed.

After I'd seen the puppies — they were beautiful, with their soft fur and velvety noses — Will took me home on the crossbar of his bike. 'Mind you don't fall off now!' his mother called after us. The snow had gone from the road so it was easy enough riding and we only had one bad wobble. Will saved us from going over just in time.

My mum was bringing in the sheets. The wind was trying to snatch them out of her hands. I helped her grab the corners and fold them. They were starchy stiff with the cold. My mum's always got

heaps of washing. (I've already decided that *I* am not going to have five children when I grow up. They dirty too many things.)

'What do you think about Mrs Ramsay wanting to go and live in Glasgow?' I asked.

'It's not a crime, wanting to live in the city.'

'You wouldn't want to though, would you?'

'Me? No. But I'm different. I've always lived in the country.' (Her dad was a shepherd.) 'I wouldn't be able to breathe in the city.'

One person's meat is another person's poison. Mrs Gordon wrote the proverb on the blackboard one day. She said we shouldn't expect everyone to be like ourselves. Think how boring that would be! Not everyone would want to go to a one-teacher school. Though I think they're daft if they don't.

In spite of my ankle I decided to go for a wee walk up the hill behind the house. From there you can see the two lochans on the other side. The water looked dark blue and still, with inky-black shadows round the edge. On the shores the moss was a sharp green where it showed through the snow. It was a bit like the colour of fresh lettuce. Beyond the moor stretched the hills, in their envelope of snow. They were turning pink in the light of the setting sun. I sighed. I wished I could paint like Mrs Smith.

It was dead quiet. I could hear only the faint sigh of the wind. There was so much space around. But I guessed there wouldn't be if all the people from

Glasgow were to come up and live here.

Bruce and Lynne were a few minutes late coming in to school on Monday morning. It wasn't like them. I wondered if they might not be coming at all.

'Maybe they're leaving for Glasgow straight away?'

'I would doubt it, Katy,' said Mrs Gordon. 'People don't move *that* quickly.'

The door opened and in came Bruce and Lynne, red in the face from running.

'Sorry we're late,' mumbled Bruce.

Lynne said, 'Mummy and Daddy were —'

'Shut up!' barked Bruce.

They sat down. The class was dead quiet. I could hear our Annie breathing through her mouth. She had a cold.

'When does he start then, Bruce?' I asked. 'Your dad – in Glasgow?'

'He's not starting.'

'He's *not* starting?'

'No. He's decided not to take the job.'

A cheer went up, hushed quickly by Mrs Gordon.

'That's very decent of your dad,' I said.

'It wasn't to save the school.' Bruce was embarrassed. 'I mean, he doesn't want the school to shut but —'

'We couldn't expect him to turn down a job because of it,' Mrs Gordon finished off for him. 'Anyway, it is none of our business why he is not taking the job.'

In spite of the teacher's time-to-close-the-subject voice, Lynne decided to let us in on the reason. She'd have told us in the playground later, anyway.

'He said three days in the city nearly killed him. He couldn't stand the noise of the traffic.'

'Don't blame him.' Danny put his hands over his ears and proceeded to make a grinding noise at the back of his throat that was meant to sound like traffic. Mrs Gordon ticked him off with a frown.

'And everything looked so tatty,' Lynne went on, 'that he couldn't wait to get back to the glen and the fresh air.'

I then asked the question which everyone else was itching to ask. 'What about your mum?'

'She's not a bit pleased!'

We thought that was what Mrs Gordon would call an understatement.

'Not one bit,' stressed Lynne, nodding her head in a knowing kind of way, like her own mum does.

Mrs Ramsay took off her high heels and put on her wellies and went out and about. She did the rounds of the houses drinking cups of tea and coffee, telling everybody how lonely and fed up she was. She said that sometimes when she was staring out of the window at the sheep on the hill she thought she'd go off her head.

Mrs McPherson said to Mairi that what Mrs Ramsay needed was a job to take her out of the house and give her something else to think about.

'Could your mum not fix up something?' I suggested. 'Your mum's a brilliant fixer.'

So Mrs McPherson took it upon herself to do some fixing. After all, she knows everybody's business in the town as well as the glen. It took her only a couple of days to arrange a part-time job for Mrs Ramsay at Will's uncle's estate agency.

'Why didn't you think of that?' I asked Will.

'Why would I think of it? I wasn't trying to find Mrs Ramsay a job!'

'I suppose you don't care if Mrs Ramsay gets a job or not! You men are all the same – that's what my mum says.'

Alison told us to stop scrapping.

The job at the estate agency was right down Mrs Ramsay's street. She loves going into other folks' houses to look them over. And she would be allowed into all the rooms, bedrooms and bathrooms too, which she doesn't usually get to see. The hours were ideal – nine to three – and the playgroup in town agreed to take Glenda. And Mrs Ramsay was to have the use of a car – she would need it for the job – so that solved the problem of her and Glenda getting up and down to Inchbeg.

'Our mum thinks her job's great,' Lynne was able to report after her first day.

Now the Ramsays stayed at school over lunchtime. Lynne didn't care for that so much.

'I liked going home for my dinner.'

'Tough beans!' I told her. 'You've got to be prepared to make some sacrifices to stop your mum going off her head.'

(Danny did a drawing of Mrs Ramsay walking about with her head off. Mrs Gordon was annoyed and made him put it in the wastepaper basket.)

With the Ramsay family settled down and sorted out, we could relax a little. We started talking as if that had also settled the matter of the school being kept open. But, as Mairi pointed out, we *still* had only fourteen pupils on the roll and the Education Committee had *still* not crumbled under the demands of our parents or ourselves.

'We're really just back to square one.'

'It's like Snakes and Ladders,' said Danny.

He was right. We had slid down a snake. And had now come up a little ladder. What *were* we to do to get up the very tall ladder that would take us to the top of the board and bring us home and dry?

FOURTEEN

SOMETHING UP-FRONT

It was Friday lunch-time, and we were having a baking sale, even though we had finished the magazine. We are always needing money for something.

The women were in a chatty mood today, more interested in talking than buying. I won't have to tell you what they were talking about.

'We simply *must* take further action,' Mrs Smith was saying. 'We've got to do something more up-front. I mean, writing letters is all very well, but it's not enough.'

'You're right,' said my mum. 'They can read the letters and throw them in the bin, can't they?'

Mrs Gordon looked a bit annoyed at that. Hadn't she spent days getting us to write letters? In our very best writing?

'Oh, I'm not saying they're *no* use —' My mum broke off to grab our Florrie's arm but she wasn't quick enough. Florrie had a whole scone crammed into her mouth and was munching. Her red cheeks bulged like a hamster's. 'I'll pay for that, Mairi. In fact, I'll take two dozen scones. They look lovely.' My mum needs to buy in dozens.

Mrs Smith, who only eats wholesome foods, decided on a banana and honey cake. I put it carefully into a bag. No shortbread or fudge for the Smiths – too much sugar. Everybody knows that sugar rots your teeth. (I love walnut fudge.)

Davie the Post was buying shortbread. He's got false teeth anyway. Maybe he did get them from eating too much sugar. But he doesn't pay any attention to Mrs Smith telling him it's bad for his heart as well. He says he's got this far without any trouble so he'll just carry on.

'So what have you in mind, Mrs Smith?' he asked. 'By up-front?'

We were all keen to hear what Mrs Smith meant by 'up-front'.

'We're not wanting to slide down any more snakes,' said Danny, who had snakes on the brain that morning. He'd written a poem about them. This is how it went:

'Slithery, slimy, slobbery snakes.

Slavery, sloppity, slidy snakes.

Don't go near them – for goodness sakes!'

Mrs Gordon had then suggested he write one about ladders. So here it is:

'Lovely, long, laddery ladders,

Lofty, looming, lengthy ladders.

Find one quick – and get away from the adders!'

(Mairi gave him 'adders'.)

'Snakes were easier to write about than ladders,' Danny said.

Mrs Gordon had pinned the poems on the wall. Our mum went over to read them. The back wall is covered with poems and stories and drawings.

'What we need,' I said, 'is a lovely, long, laddery ladder.'

Blackberry's mother nodded, 'You're right, Katy. We've got to put on a show of support for the school. A demonstration of some kind.'

'We could lie down in the road,' I suggested. I'd seen some people doing it on television.

'They wouldn't pay any attention,' said Will. 'Who'd *see* us if we were to lie down in the road here?'

'We'd have to go to Edinburgh,' said Mrs Smith.

'Edinburgh!' I whooped.

'Though perhaps we wouldn't lie in the road!'

'I want to lie in the road,' said Danny, spreading his arms out wide and closing his eyes, pretending to be dead.

Mrs Smith was getting warmed up. 'We could call at the Secretary of State for Scotland's office and hand in a petition. And carry placards to attract attention. That's what it's all about – being noticed.'

'I want a card to carry,' said Annie.

'Me too!' cried Blackberry. 'Mummy, can I get a card?'

By now the whole school was clustered round the baking table and Mrs Smith. Mrs Gordon had to hold on to the end of the table to stop it from toppling.

'Mind the raspberry sponge!' cried Mrs Scott. (She probably didn't fancy having to clean it off the floor.)

Mrs Gordon told us to calm down. We were fizzing like Hallowe'en sparklers. We hushed to listen to Mrs Smith, who seemed to know all about demonstrations. She was talking about publicity and press releases.

The raspberry sponge was sliding again. I grabbed it, just in time. I was hoping my mum would buy it. (She did. It tasted yummy.)

'How would we get to Edinburgh?' asked Bruce.

'We could hire a bus.'

'It would have to be on a Saturday, wouldn't it?' said Mrs Scott. 'So that it wouldn't interfere with school.'

'How would we pay for the bus?' asked Mairi.

'We can raise the money, stupid!' I cried. As far as I was concerned, I was already half-way to Edinburgh in my head. A wee thing like money wasn't going to stop us.

'What do *you* think, Mrs Gordon?' asked my mum. 'Would you go along with it?'

Mrs Gordon had been saying very little. She had her thoughtful look on.

'Well ... Yes, I would!' She seemed suddenly to

make up her mind. 'We've got our backs up against the wall, after all.'

'That's why we need to do something up-front,' I said.

FIFTEEN

GETTING READY

The next three weeks were hectic. We Big Ones stayed on after school to write press releases, make placards and posters and organise a raffle. The raffle was to raise money for the bus. Danny was counted as a Big One since he's a Five and half-way to being a Six and we needed all hands on deck once again.

Everyone in the glen donated something for the raffle: fruit cakes, bottles of whisky and sherry, tins of shortbread, boxes of chocolates, sweaters (Mrs Scott's got a knitting machine), a frozen salmon, ornaments, pieces of china and pottery. The butcher who comes round in his van on Fridays promised us a haggis and a haunch of venison. Mrs Smith gave one of her own paintings. It's a picture of the Findie in winter, with the peaty, amber-coloured water racing over the flat grey stones in the river bed. At first we couldn't make out what it was, but after we'd had it up on the wall for a few days we began to see that it was the river.

We were each given several books of raffle tickets to sell. It wasn't all that easy to sell them in the glen. Well, we don't have many neighbours, do we? And most of them have children of their own.

On Saturday morning Mrs MacDonald took us

six Big Ones into town in her estate car to do a bit of selling there. (We had to hang on to our seats with both hands. She drives as if she owns the whole road, and swings from one side to the other. Only Sam could sleep through a ride like that.)

She dropped us off outside the Tolbooth, then she went to do some shopping.

We propped up the placard that we'd brought with us. It said: PLEASE HELP SAVE GLEN FINDIE PRIMARY SCHOOL. Soon people began to stop. Everyone we spoke to was sympathetic. They said we were quite right to protest. And some of them gave us donations as well as buying raffle tickets. We did a brisk trade.

Afterwards we went to a café and had Coke and chocolate biscuits (from our own money) and counted up the morning's takings. We sat in the window where we could see all the folk going past with their shopping bags. The town's only small as towns go, according to Mrs Gordon: it has a population of twenty thousand. To us that's a lot of people, and they all seemed to be out shopping that Saturday morning.

We saw Mrs MacDonald on the other side of the road dragging Sam on a lead behind her. Whenever she stopped to speak to someone – as she often did – he took the opportunity to lie down and rest his face on his paws.

'It's good fun this,' remarked Danny, slurping up the last of his Coke. 'The town mightn't be so bad after all.'

We rounded on him. He wasn't suggesting that it wouldn't be so bad if we had to come to the school in the town, was he? And leave Glen Findie?

'Course not! But this café's OK.'

*

Back at school, the preparations continued. Mrs Smith came in to help us with the placards. Everyone in the school, big or small, would be given one to carry.

Here are some of the slogans we painted on:

HANDS OFF OUR SCHOOL!

DON'T SHUT US DOWN!

KEEP GLEN FINDIE OPEN

WE LOVE GLEN FINDIE P. SCHOOL

NO TO CLOSURE!

HANDS OFF GLEN FINDIE!

PROTECT OUR CHILDREN'S HERITAGE

SMALL IS BEAUTIFUL

Mr Smith was organising the bus. He'd booked a forty-seater. Some people were going in their own cars and the Johnsons and the MacDonalds would take the extras in their estate cars. All of us McCrees were coming, plus our Auntie Jean and Uncle Jimmy and two cousins who live over the hill in the next glen.

This is the list of people who put down their names:

14 schoolchildren
10 former pupils now at secondary school
6 Under Fives
Mr and Mrs Gordon
Mrs Gordon's sister and her family who were to come from Dundee to join us in Edinburgh
Rev. and Mrs MacDonald
Dr and Mrs Begg
Miss Graham, the visiting music teacher, and her boyfriend Alec
Mr and Mrs McCree plus 4 relatives
Mr and Mrs Johnson
Mr Johnson's brother and his wife (the estate agents) plus Helen
Mrs McPherson
(Mr McPherson wouldn't go to Edinburgh unless at gun-point, he said, and none of us wanted to have to go that far to persuade him! Mairi was a bit embarrassed that her dad wouldn't come, but Mrs Gordon said she shouldn't be. We all knew her dad felt unhappy anywhere outside the glen.)

Mr and Mrs Smith (six of their friends would
    join us in Edinburgh)
Mr and Mrs Ramsay and Glenda
Mrs Scott (Mr would be away – he's an offshore
    oil worker at Aberdeen)
Mr Simpson (Mrs has a new baby)
Mr McBean (Mrs would mind the shop)
Davie the Post
Mungo the Bus and Mrs Mungo
Jimmy the Buckets and Mrs Jimmy
Lachie the shepherd who lives at the head of the
    glen
Two teachers from the primary school in the
    town and two from the secondary

'It'll be a good turn out,' said Mrs MacDonald,
when she'd finished reading out the names. She'd
gone round collecting them. (Most people don't like
to say no to her. She'll say, 'Will I put you down for
it?' and already she'll be writing your name on her
list.)
    'Is Sam not coming?' asked Blackberry.
    'Of course Sam's coming.'
    'Goes without saying,' said I.
    'We couldn't leave you behind, could we, old
boy?' Mrs MacDonald tickled him behind the ear
with her toe.
    He opened one eye, then closed it again.
    'You'll need to keep him on a lead,' said Elspeth.

'Don't worry, I will!'

'Can we bring Jemima?' asked Hector.

'I think not!' His mother killed that idea quickly. Otherwise we could end up looking like a travelling pet shop.

Mr Smith got an interview on BBC Radio Scotland. It was on one of those chat shows where they put on a piece of music and after it's over the presenter talks to somebody in the news. Suddenly Glen Findie was news!

Mrs Gordon put on the radio so that we could hear Mr Smith. We sat very still and quiet to listen. Even Blackberry didn't say, 'That was my daddy,' until he'd done his bit and the music had come back on.

Mr Smith spoke terribly well, we were really proud of him. He talked about the school and its history and said what a happy family we were and how well we were taught and what a creative atmosphere we had to learn in and that it would be a scandal if it were to be closed down. An absolute scandal.

He then said that anyone would be welcome to join us and we would be in Charlotte Square in Edinburgh on Saturday at twelve noon.

SIXTEEN

TWELVE NOON

It was still dark when we left Glen Findie. We had balloons on the bus and coloured streamers which we trailed out of the windows. On the back window we had taped a poster which said:

SAVE GLEN FINDIE PRIMARY SCHOOL CAMPAIGN

Mrs Gordon had given us a talk the day before. We were *not* to get too excited or make too much noise. We were to be on our *very* best behaviour as all eyes would be on us.

It was difficult to be *very* quiet on the bus. We couldn't stop talking and laughing. After a while when the noise began to get too much Mrs Gordon clapped her hands and said, 'What about a song?' She started us on *Old MacDonald's Farm*. Then we had *This Old Man*.

We sang for the rest of the way, except when we were eating. We'd brought packed lunches. 'Enough to feed half the population of Edinburgh!' said Mr Gordon.

When we got to the outskirts of Edinburgh, we quietened down and glued ourselves to the windows.

Some of us had never been there before – none of us McCrees had. There are too many of us to go places.

'Is that Arthur's Seat?' Danny pointed at the crouching, lion-shaped hill which looks down over the city.

'It is.' Mr Smith nodded. 'And at its feet you have the Queen's Park and Holyrood Palace. The hill does look like a lion, doesn't it?'

'I want to go up the lion,' shouted Jamie.

'I want to go to the palace,' cried Hector.

'We'll see, we'll see!' said Mrs Gordon. She was smiling. 'Perhaps afterwards. First things first.'

She'd promised that after we'd done our demon-
strating we could go on a tour of the city and see
some of its sights. That way we'd kill two birds with
one stone. Jamie had then said he didn't think you
were allowed to throw stones at birds. He'd said our
mum had given him a row when he'd thrown a stone
at a nasty big blackbird who was eating the bread
he'd put out for the tits.

'There's the castle!' I shouted, jumping up. I was
the first to spot it.

There was no mistaking the castle. There it sat on
its stark, steep rock above Princes Street Gardens

looking fierce and ancient. It is very old, of course. It dates back to the eleventh century. We know about its history. We know about the battles that have taken place there during the times of William Wallace and Robert the Bruce; how the English would capture the castle and then the Scots take it back. The fighting had been fierce. Looking at the castle, you could believe it.

The sight of it made us all feel excited. We were here, in Edinburgh, we really were!

The bus turned off Princes Street, up into Charlotte Square. It's a square with a garden in the middle surrounded by very fine houses, most of which are now offices. Mr Smith gave us a running commentary. On the far side – at Number Five – is Bute House, the residence of the Secretary of State for Scotland. Not that he would probably be there. We were disappointed when we heard he wouldn't. That didn't matter, apparently. The main thing was to hand in our petition, and to be seen doing it.

The bus parked and we got out, in orderly fashion, carrying our placards. Nobody pushed or shoved. We waited on the pavement, then all together, with Mr Gordon acting as traffic controller, we crossed the wide street to the pavement in front of Number Five. There was a plaque saying 'National Trust for Scotland' on the black wrought-iron railings. Mrs Gordon explained that the National Trust lets the Secretary of State use the house as his Scottish

136

residence. Most of the time, though, he is in London.

A few people had collected already. Dr and Mrs Begg had arrived. That was good as Dr Begg could see to anyone who fainted or didn't feel well. The minister and his wife and Sam had also made it down safely. Mrs MacDonald had Sam on a long lead and he was wandering up and down sniffing in the gutter. The Edinburgh air must have made him feel young again. Mrs Gordon's sister and her family from Dundee were waiting to welcome us. They gave us a big wave. And we recognised the Smiths' friends by their clothes – they looked like artists. They weren't wearing their best going-out clothes with their shoes polished, like we were. (They looked a bit scruffy, to tell the truth.)

And there was a man with two big cameras slung over his shoulders leaning against the black railings. He was from the Press. *Scotland on Sunday*, he said. We were beginning to feel very important!

Then a couple of policemen came strolling round the corner. Just to keep an eye on things, they told Mrs Gordon. She had had to get permission from the police for us to be in Charlotte Square. (You're supposed to do that if more than six people gather together in a public place, though Mairi says she's seen more than double that standing on a corner in the town after school. Mrs Gordon says it depends on what you're gathered for. If it's to have a

137

demonstration, then you have to tell the police.)

Mr Gordon and Mr Smith arranged us on the pavement so that the different slogans on the placards would be spread around. They separated Annie and Blackberry who were both carrying SMALL IS BEAUTIFUL.

Even while they were doing their arranging, more people were arriving. Some seemed to know about us, others had caught sight of our placards and were curious. One or two of the mothers like Mrs McPherson and my mum and one or two of the pupils (like Alison and me) filled them in on what was going on. Most of them decided to stick around to give us their support and see what would happen. It wasn't long before the pavement was swarming and the crowd was spilling over into the road.

And then the television arrived!

A big van with Scottish Television on its side had come swerving into the kerb. Imagine, *we* were going to be on the telly! We moved our feet back from the kerb-edge. A number of people got out of the van carrying long trailing wires and lights and a big camera mounted on a stand which could roll along the pavement. It was now ten minutes to twelve.

In the next few minutes three more men and one woman from the Press arrived. Two were photographers, two reporters. Then came two people from BBC Radio Scotland.

'So you see, children,' said Mrs MacDonald, 'it

was worth all the effort with the press releases.'

We'd argued over the wording of them for hours. Mrs Gordon had told us not to be too sensational. You couldn't say, as Danny had suggested, that one of the most terrible crimes in Scottish history was about to be committed. That would be going well over the top! We'd had to be reasonable and set our our reasons calmly and clearly. People don't listen if you go over the top, said Mrs MacDonald.

By twelve o'clock several hundred people had collected. One reporter said he estimated the crowd to be five or six hundred. I thought it was more like a thousand. Whatever the number was, it looked like an *enormous* crowd to us. We'd never seen anything like it before. The television camera had started to roll.

Mr Smith cleared a path up to the front door of Number Five and the other men helped keep the crowd back. Then Mrs Gordon, holding the petition aloft so that the television and the Press could see it, went forward and mounted the five steps up to the brown door. We fell in behind her: first the Sevens, then the Sixes, right down to the two Ones. A man with a microphone on a long lead kept pace with Mrs Gordon and stayed at her side.

She pressed the bell. They must have been waiting for us in their Corridor of Power for the door opened at once. A man in a grey suit came out on to the step. He was smiling and he spoke very politely.

139

Well, he would, wouldn't he, when he was going to be on the telly? He wouldn't say, 'I think we should close your silly little school,' and snarl at us.

'Good morning. Or should I say good afternoon?'

Mrs Gordon was very polite, too. 'Good afternoon,' she replied. She was wearing her best dark-green suit and cream silk blouse and was looking very smart. 'We've come from Glen Findie Primary School to protest about the proposed closure of our school.'

At that moment Sam raised his head and howled. We hadn't heard him make as much noise for a long time. It was as if he was making his protest too. Alison and I, who were partners, grinned at one another.

Mrs Gordon was saying her next bit. 'We would like to give you this petition to pass to the Secretary of State for Scotland.'

'I shall certainly do that.' Still smiling, the man took the petition from Mrs Gordon's hand. Cameras flashed. 'Good day to you all.'

The door closed. We turned and faced the Press. The cameras went off again. One of the photographers grouped us on the steps, placing Annie and Blackberry together in front.

'You've got to put Sam in,' I said.

Mrs MacDonald brought Sam over and he collapsed on top of the two Wee Ones' feet. He must have been feeling worn out with all the excitement.

Then the photographer knelt down, held up his camera, asked us to say 'Cheese' and flash! the bulb lit up again.

After that the BBC Radio reporters interviewed those of us who would be willing to say a few words.

141

All right, so what if I did volunteer? Somebody has to do these things. And I don't mind talking, especially when it's for a good cause. Mairi and Alison and Will said a few words as well.

The crowd started to drift away. By a quarter to one it was all over.

SEVENTEEN

WAITING

Mr McBean videoed the news report and on Sunday afternoon a crowd of us went down to the village to see it. We crammed into the little living-room in the back shop.

'There's Mrs Gordon!' yelled Danny, jumping up and stabbing the screen with his finger.

'Sit down!' we yelled. 'Keep back!'

We'd almost missed it. The door of Number Five Charlotte Square was opening and the man with the smile was stretching out his hand to take our petition. Now the camera swung away and showed us grouped together on the pavement. And then we vanished. We'd only been on for about a minute.

'Is that all?' wailed Lynne.

'Wait now!' Mr Mcbean held up his hand. 'I'll run it through again.'

'We could only expect a short report,' said Mrs Gordon.

'The main thing,' said Mr Smith, 'is that we got it.'

Mr McBean ran the film through another six times. It was funny seeing ourselves on the screen.

We didn't look quite like ourselves. That was probably because of the good clothes and our hair being so neat and tidy. Danny had put on some of our dad's hair cream and his head looked like a seal's that had just come out of the water.

'It was a great day though, wasn't it?' I sighed.

We felt a bit flat now that it was over and the waiting had begun. We were tired too. Saturday had been a long day. Most of us had fallen asleep (not me) on the bus coming home.

But we'd enjoyed the day. Every single bit of it. Going to the castle and the palace and the Museum of Childhood and the funny wee closes off the Royal Mile. They're the narrow dark alleyways that run into the back courts between the high tenements.

We wrote it all up of course when we went back to school (what else would you expect!), and drew pictures. Danny's imagination took off. He wrote five pages about the closes. He imagined that he was living in the Middle Ages and footpads and murderers were skulking about with dirks at the ready. He began, 'As dusk fell, terrifying screams could be heard ...'

Annie and Blackberry had liked the Museum of Childhood best, especially the doll's houses and the china dolls in their old-fashioned dresses. They'd wanted to stay and play with them. It's funny because Annie never plays with dolls at home. She prefers toy tractors and dump trucks. But I suppose those dolls were special. (I could have played with them myself!)

The *very* best bit of the day, though, was giving in the petition, with all the people there and the television cameras rolling and the flashbulbs popping.

*

The next two weeks seemed more like two years, while we waited for a reaction from the Corridors of Power. The most exciting thing that happened was that I won Mrs Smith's picture in the raffle!

('Exciting for *you* maybe,' says Alison.)

I love the painting. I've got it on the wall of my room where I can see it from my bed. And I've put it too high for either Florrie or Annie to reach. I don't want their sticky fingers on it. I have to share a bedroom with them. Unfortunately. They're always touching my things.

('This is a diversion,' says Mairi. 'And nothing to do with the story.' It's got everything to do with it, I tell her. I only have Mrs Smith's picture *because* of the raffle. And we only had the raffle *because* we had to raise funds for the bus. Mairi says she thinks I should get on with the story anyway but I tell her there was not a lot to get on with at that point. How can you write about *waiting*? 'That's a challenge,' says Mrs Gordon.)

So, all right, we were waiting. Not very patiently. Even the hands of the clock seemed to be moving more slowly. The second hand looked heavy, as if it couldn't be bothered hauling itself right up to the top. Mrs Gordon agreed that it did seem rather reluctant. But it had always been like that – we'd just not noticed before.

We had plenty of school work to get on with, but nothing special to do. The magazine was finished,

146

and all the copies sold. We were waiting to hear the result of *The Scotsman* competition as well. That wouldn't come until the third week in March. We were still in February and having flurries of snow from time to time, though not enough to get a holiday. (Much as we like our school, we don't mind holidays, either.) Spring seemed ages away, almost unimaginable. The earth looked dead and the trees, apart from the pines, were as bare as sticks.

We were suffering from anti-climax, Mrs Gordon explained, after all the excitement. (It means being down in the dumps.) She wrote the word on the blackboard. Blackberry copied it into her jotter. She likes words with 'x's in. As we've already told you, she can't wait to be a Six. She used to write it 'Siks', but has learned not to now.

All the Edinburgh stories were written up and pinned on the wall. It was back to normal in the class-room.

'I hate normal,' I said.

Mrs Gordon did what she could to take our minds off it. We could tell she was trying. She read aloud to us more than usual. She started us on new projects. The weather turned mild for a few days, though we weren't daft enough to believe it would stay that way. Not yet. Not before April. Or even May. Danny found the first tiny crocus spear under the old lilac tree.

'You see, children,' said Mrs Gordon, 'spring *is* on its way. The ground is beginning to stir, even if ever so slowly.'

'I hope they start stirring in the Corridors of Power,' I said.

Maybe they heard me, for three days later, a letter arrived from the Director of Education himself. It was addressed to Mrs Gordon *and* the pupils of Glen Findie Primary School.

Davie waited to see what was in it. Mrs Gordon slit the top of the envelope with her paper knife. We gathered round her table.

'No pushing now, children!'

'I feel sick,' said Alison.

Mrs Gordon drew out a single sheet of white paper.

'I am coming to visit you,' the Director of Education had written.

He was coming on Thursday, the day after tomorrow.

EIGHTEEN

DIRECT FROM THE
CORRIDORS OF POWER

We tidied the shelves, took down the drawings that were curling at the edges and put up new ones. Mrs Scott cleaned the windows, which she does only once in a blue moon. (Have you ever seen a blue moon? Blackberry says she has.) And Mrs McPherson brought us some daffodils from a shop in the town to decorate the window sills.

We put on our good clothes again and re-polished our shoes. Danny didn't cream his head this time, after we'd told him he'd looked like a seal on the telly. I wore my new red corduroy skirt and tied my hair back with a red ribbon.

'You with a ribbon on, Katy McCree!' said Will, taking care to dance out of my way.

'Look at you!'

He was wearing his kilt with a shirt and a *tie* and an Aran sweater. Bruce had his kilt on, too. So did Danny and Jamie. Hector had on a bow-tie. He's fond of bow-ties, is Hector. This one was yellow with green dinosaurs on it.

We felt more nervous than we had when going to Edinburgh. Then there'd been a great big bus-load of us and we'd had our mothers and fathers along and we could sing and make a noise. Now there was just us and Mrs Gordon and we were quiet. (Mrs Gordon was a bit nervous herself, though I'm sure she wouldn't have admitted it.)

We had never had a visit from the Director of Education before.

'Will it be a man or a woman?' asked Mary.

'A man, of course,' said Bruce.

'Why shouldn't it be a woman?' I demanded.

'No reason why not,' agreed Mrs Gordon. 'I don't think there are any yet, though. Not in Scotland, at any rate.'

'I'll be a Director of Education when I grow up and I'll open lots and lots of little schools like ours!'

'You wouldn't like it in the Corridors of Power,' said Will.

'Want to bet?'

We were having a rather noisy discussion of what it would be like to be in the Corridors of Power when the Director's black car glided past the window.

'It's him!' shouted Alison.

We sat down at once and opened our books. We bent our heads and got on with sums, or at least pretended to. It was difficult to concentrate when we were waiting to hear what our fate would be. Well, who could do *sums* when that was hanging over them?

Mrs Gordon went out to greet him. We listened to their conversation going on in the outer vestibule. Mrs Gordon asked him if he'd had a pleasant journey and she hoped the roads hadn't been too bad. Not at all, he answered. He'd enjoyed the drive. The countryside looked beautiful up here at all times of the year. And so on. I rolled my eyes at Alison, who looked as if she was feeling sick again. The two of them sounded as if they could go on out there for hours. We just wanted him to come in and tell us yes or no!

'I'm needing,' said Annie.

'No, you are not!' I whispered. I had to be quite fierce with her, so that she wouldn't say it again. She had been told *not* to ask out to the toilet unless she was desperate.

At last, the classroom door opened, and Mrs Gordon brought in the Director. As we expected, he was wearing a navy-blue suit. He'd cleaned his shoes, too. The toe-caps were shining.

We pushed back our chairs and stood up.

'Good morning, sir.'

'Good morning, boys and girls. Please be seated.'

Jamie dropped a marble as he was sitting down. A red and green mottled marble. He'd swopped it at break with Hector for a stick of chewing gum. The little glistening glass ball went spinning across the floor towards the Director! We held our breath.

The Director put out one shiny, black shoe and

151

stopped the marble in its tracks. Then he bent down and lifted it up between his finger and thumb and held it against the light.

'Pretty things, marbles.' He was smiling. We let out our breath.

He laid the marble on Mrs Gordon's desk. Jamie looked relieved. He might have been asked to go out and claim it.

'I've heard a great deal about you and your school,' said the Director. 'And read about you – in the newspapers!'

Mrs Gordon asked if he would like to see some of our work. I don't know why she had to ask him for of course he said that he would. They set off on a tour round the walls.

They took an awful long time going round. He kept stopping to read the stories and poems and then he'd ask who'd written this or drawn that? We each put up our hands in turn.

'Excellent! First class!'

If he thought our work was so brilliant, then surely he wouldn't want to close us down? Could we count on that? On the other hand he might say, 'If you can do this kind of work here, you can do it anywhere!'

At last he went back to stand in front of Mrs Gordon's table.

'You all seem to be very happy at school?'

'Yes, sir,' we chorused.

'What is it you like so much about your school?'

Annie's hand shot up. We groaned quietly, inside our heads. We knew what she'd say.

'Are the toilets *so* special?' he asked. A little smile was hanging around the edges of his mouth. At least I hoped it was a smile.

Annie nodded. 'They're little and I can reach them.'

Blackberry's hand was now waving for attention.

'Our toilet at home's bigger,' she announced, and looked round, pleased with herself. 'And it's got a real wooden seat. My mummy and daddy don't like plastic.'

'So what else is good apart from the toilets?' The director was smiling again.

We made sure the Wee Ones didn't get a word in now. In turn, the rest of us told him why we thought our school was special. I don't have to spell it out – you'll know by now.

'Sounds like good fun to me,' he commented when we'd finished.

'It is,' I said. '*Great* fun.'

Would he think fun was important?

'But we do learn a lot too,' Mairi added anxiously. 'It's just that we *enjoy* it.'

'What else could you want from a school?' he asked.

'Nothing!' we cried.

'I think I must tell you now that we have decided *not* to close your school!'

For a moment we couldn't quite take it in. He'd said it so calmly, when we felt anything but calm. Then his words began to sink into our soggy brains. They'd decided *not* to close the school. That *was* what he had said, wasn't it?

We cheered. He seemed like a man who wouldn't mind a bit of cheering.

P.S.

We have just had a phone call from *The Scotsman* offices in Edinburgh to tell us that we have won the award for the Best School Magazine in Scotland! For the whole of Scotland. Primary and secondary. Can you believe it? We hardly can.

We are absolutely over the moon about it – blue or any other colour. In fact, we think there could be a rainbow moon tonight. We can't stop talking and Mrs Gordon isn't even trying to stop us. We're talking with exclamation marks.

'Imagine – the *best* in Scotland!'

'And there are only fourteen of us!'

'Some of the schools must have more than two hundred pupils!'

'Some will have over a thousand!'

'Some probably have five thousand!'

'Don't exaggerate, Katy McCree!'

Mrs Gordon says that we must have a celebration. We all agree! We love celebrations. We put our books into our desks and shut the lids and Mrs Gordon takes Alison and Mairi with her into the house. They come back carrying a couple of big bottles of apple juice, paper cups, and a tin of biscuits with a picture of Edinburgh castle on its lid.

'I seen that castle,' says Jamie.

'Saw,' I say.

'We all saw it,' says Lynne. 'Didn't we, Mrs Gordon?'

'You certainly did.'

Mairi pours the juice into the cups and Alison and I give them out. Will takes round the biscuit tin.

Mrs Gordon raises her cup. 'Here's to Glen Findie Primary School!'

'And may it never ever close!' I cry.

'To *us*!'

We get to our feet and drink.

'Winning's good fun,' says Annie. 'Specially when you get juice.'

'They must be pleased now that they didn't close us down!' says Will.

'They'd look right idiots if they had, wouldn't they?' I say. '*Right* idiots!'

'Maybe the Director'll come back and see us another time,' says Danny.

He may well do. He seemed to enjoy his visit. He even stayed to lunch and afterwards had a game of shinty with us in the field. He took off his jacket and loosened his tie. And he didn't seem to mind that he got his toe-caps muddied.

Before we finish our juice the phone rings again and this time it's *him*. He wants to say, 'Well done,

everybody! And very well deserved!' Mrs Gordon
lets him say it. When she puts down the receiver, she
passes on his message.

Then she picks up a brand-new stick of yellow
chalk and writes on the blackboard:

SMALL IS BEAUTIFUL!